CANDLE FACE CHRONICLES

THE LOST SOULS
[BOOK TWO]

Arthur Mills

CANDLE FACE CHRONICLES

THE LOST SOULS
[BOOK TWO]

ARTHUR MILLS

Branching Plot Books

2025

ISBN: Paperback   978-1-7363392-5-1
eBook for Kindle   978-1-7363392-6-8

BOOKS BY ARTHUR MILLS

- The Empty Lot Next Door
- The Crawl Space
- Friend or Foe
- Co-Author
- Candle Face Chronicles: The Lost Souls [Book One]
- Candle Face Chronicles: The Lost Souls [Book Two]
- Candle Face Chronicles: Isabel: The Forgotten Daughter of La Llorona [Book Three]
- The Haunted Handbook
- The Legend of Mara Flores

DEDICATION

To my readers,

This book, like the first, is dedicated to you. Your commitment, curiosity, and compassion have brought hope to the Lost Souls seeking peace. Every clue you consider carries the possibility of justice and some resolution for the people Candle Face and her followers killed.

These Lost Souls depend on your ideas, courage, and determination to listen to their stories and help them find the rest they deserve. Through your engagement with this book and its interactive elements, you're part of the effort to bring attention to the evil that Candle Face has spread.

Thank you for being part of this investigation. Together, we may still help these Lost Souls find the peace they so desperately need.

THE LOST SOULS

Beneath Candle Face's cruel domain,
The Lost Souls cry, trapped in pain.

Their voices plead through the endless night,
For readers brave to bring them light.

Your courage sparks a guiding flame,
To break their chains and end her reign.

With every clue, her grip grows weak,
And peace draws closer, the freedom they seek.

One day she'll fall, her shadow erased,
And the Lost Souls will find their place.

KEY TO UNDERSTANDING

To fully understand this book, readers should be familiar with my memoir *The Empty Lot Next Door*, which was inspired by actual ghostly events in Austin, Texas. That book gives readers the background needed to understand the events and references that shape *Candle Face Chronicles: The Lost Souls [Book Two]*. Without that context, some parts of this book may not have the same impact. For that reason, reading *The Empty Lot Next Door* first is strongly recommended.

To purchase *The Empty Lot Next Door*, please visit Amazon

- Paperback: https://amzn.to/46lCovb
- eBook for Kindle: https://amzn.to/44YFww4
- Audiobook for Audible: https://amzn.to/40RIHH1

TABLE OF CONTENTS

INTRODUCTION

As Candle Face grew more vicious, it became clear that my investigation into the Lost Souls was only beginning. The first book in this series, *Candle Face Chronicles: The Lost Souls [Book One]*, showed the scope of Candle Face's terror. This second volume moves further into the network of her followers and the Lost Souls who reach out for justice.

The testimonies of Candle Face's victims have intensified and grown more complex. The spirits who find their way to me have grown bolder, and their messages have become more detailed and specific. Names have started to emerge, along with histories, connections, and unfinished stories that demand resolution. As their testimonies unfold, so do the clues that might lead us to their remains, their killers, and a clearer understanding of Candle Face herself.

Book Two chronicles the next phase. Candle Face's methods grow more insidious, and the network of her followers becomes more tangled. The spirits that visit me bring testimonies of tragedy, betrayal, manipulation, and a disturbing look into the minds of those who serve her. Some followers are driven by fear. Others act out of twisted devotion. They carry out her will with horrifying precision.

The growing collaboration with you, the readers, sets this book apart. Here, you'll find stories and calls to action. The spirits' testimonies contain hidden messages and cryptic clues. Your engagement is vital. Piecing together how someone was killed, identifying a killer, and tracing the steps that led a soul to Candle Face's Lair all require close attention and sound judgment.

As these stories continue, the focus shifts. *Book One* concentrates on understanding the phenomena and establishing contact with the Lost Souls. *Book Two* pushes us into action. The search for justice becomes more urgent, and the need to protect the fugitives, those spirits who have managed to escape Candle Face's Lair, becomes more pressing. Alongside these efforts, we must confront Candle Face herself as she seeks to draw more followers under her control.

I ask you to join me again in this investigation. Together, we may still bring peace to the Lost Souls and perhaps find a way to end Candle Face's terror. The Lost Souls are counting on us.

CANDLE FACE VICTIM #28: THE TORMENT OF BETRAYAL

April 30, 2024

Retirement offers its share of surprises. Some days, I find myself occupied with household chores. Other days, I'm lost in endless scrolling on Facebook and YouTube. Today was one of those days. I must've spent 12 hours lounging on my couch in my boxers, watching video after video.

Around 4:00 a.m., I heard footsteps descending the stairs. Assuming it was my son, I didn't look up at first. Then, the sound of a woman clearing her throat made me pause. It seemed she wanted to be noticed. Glancing up, I saw a woman in her early thirties with a man's tie knotted tightly around her neck. I wondered if this spirit would attempt to attack me, as others have in the past.

Sensing she had a story to tell, I sat up and pulled out my notebook filled with paranormal investigation forms, ready to document her testimony. She took this as her signal to begin and spoke in a scratchy, high-pitched voice.

> Our conversations had become so repetitive, I could predict every word before he said it. Each day felt like a rerun of the last. Same phrases. Same lifeless kisses that barely even registered. We were stuck in this endless loop, going through the motions of a marriage that had long since lost its spark.
>
> "Planning for Christmas shopping?" my husband asked as we sat in a dimly lit restaurant, the clatter of dishes and the sounds of nearby conversations filling the room. His voice lacked genuine interest, as though the question was merely a line in an overused script.
>
> I dipped my fingers into my purse and pulled out my lipstick with a practiced motion. Without making eye contact, I replied, "Trying to beat the holiday rush."
>
> We rose from our seats at the same time. "Love you," he said, a phrase that felt as hollow as the restaurant on a Tuesday night.
>
> I replied, "Love you too," and we exited the restaurant, his hand slipping into mine out of habit. I drove him back to work, our conversation drifting into silence, broken only by the sound of traffic.

Once he closed the car door behind him, I sped away, driven by an urgency only I could understand. My destination was a small, plain apartment in North Austin. It wasn't much. It had become my escape. My boyfriend was thoughtful, passionate, and alive in a way I hadn't felt in years. He made me laugh. He challenged me. He reminded me I could feel something other than numb.

When I walked in, the familiar smell of his cologne hit me first, musky, with just a hint of the old books he loved to read. "Finally," he said, pulling me into a hug. His voice had this way of grounding me, like nothing else mattered when I was with him.

But something felt off that night. He was holding me, and his grip felt different. When I pulled back to look at him, his eyes were glossy, like he was about to cry.

"You shouldn't have ridiculed her," he said, barely above a whisper.

"Who?" I asked.

Then the room changed. A hot breeze swept through the room, and the shadows on the walls started moving, almost like they had minds of their own. In the middle of it all, I saw her. A figure standing there, her grin twisted and her eyes empty.

I froze. My boyfriend started chanting in some language I didn't recognize, his voice shaking as the shadows seemed to respond to him.

"Why are you doing this?" I asked, my voice breaking.

His face crumpled. "She requires devotion, and you don't have it. I don't have a choice."

The air in the room grew so hot I felt like I couldn't breathe. And then, I heard it. The laughter. Low at first, then louder, surrounding me, mocking me. I tried to scream, but my voice got caught in my throat. I knew then there was no way out.

I learned later that weeks had passed, and my absence remained unexplained. Rumors about my disappearance swirled. My husband and boyfriend eventually found themselves face-to-face in a secluded bar on the outskirts of Austin.

Taking a gulp from his drink, my boyfriend broke the silence. "I didn't ask for this," he admitted.

My husband's response was cold, devoid of remorse. "It was either her or us."

"Faith has power," my boyfriend said, staring at the swirling patterns in his glass. "Doubt gets you killed."

The woman tugged at the tie around her neck, grimacing as it tightened. Her eyes met mine, and her expression held pain and understanding.

"Don't let this discourage you," she said, her voice softer now. "Most of us aren't like that. If you're a jerk in life, you're a jerk in death too. That doesn't change. The good ones, the ones who were kind and gave a damn, stay that way too."

She paused, maybe trying to put into words what she wanted me to understand. "Look, death amplifies who we are. People who were kind when they were alive keep doing it after. They become the kind of spirits who want to guide and help. People who were selfish, angry, or cruel don't magically turn into saints just because they're dead."

She gestured to the faint shimmer of the portal in the corner of the room. "You'll meet all kinds. Some of us bring misery, sure. Some of us just want to help where we can. So when you meet one of us, try to see who we were."

CANDLE FACE VICTIM #29: LOSING FAITH IN CANDLE FACE

May 12, 2024

As I settled onto the couch, the weight of the day's worries began to lift, if only slightly. Something made me open my eyes, and when I did, I noticed shadows flickering against the far wall, like the dim light had suddenly become shy. That's when I saw him. My next Lost Soul.

He appeared near the window, his form vague and shimmering. He stood there silently, watching me, like he was trying to figure out how I'd react. He clearly had something to share, some unfinished business that had brought him to my living room. I sat up, and he walked over and sat beside me. The moment my eyes met his, he began.

I first heard the stories of Candle Face on the corner of Congress Avenue and Sixth Street in Austin, TX. A group of fellow homeless folks were gathered around a light post and bench, their eyes haunted as they spoke about a ghostly girl who hunted down anyone who dared to laugh at her existence. I didn't buy it for a second, so I pushed for more.

The group was led by a woman with piercing blue eyes who talked about Candle Face with fear and reverence. She said the ghost was once a young girl who died in a horrible fire, her face left disfigured. Now, she roamed Austin's streets, punishing skeptics who didn't take her story seriously.

I couldn't help myself. I laughed and called it nonsense. "A ghost that attacks non-believers?" I mocked. "Come on."

Her expression turned cold. "Mock her, and you'll see for yourself," she warned. "But you'll regret it. She'll show you, but the cost will be more than you can imagine."

That night, under Interstate 35, I lay in my tent trying to forget her words. Then I heard it: a faint, childlike voice calling my name. My heart started pounding. I sat up, and that's when I saw her.

Candle Face.

She was horrifying. Her face charred and twisted, her eyes hollow and lifeless. She just stood there, staring at me. In her hand, she rolled a needle between her burnt fingers, like she was deciding what to do with it.

"Come with me," she said in a sad tone.

Suddenly, the world around me shifted. Austin was gone, replaced by some nightmarish version of itself, a city twisted by fire. As I followed her, she started talking, her voice shifting between innocent and commanding. "I want believers who will embrace my story, spread it, make it part of their lives."

She told me that, to those who believed, she was their guardian, offering comfort to people drowning in their pain. "For those who have faith in me," she said, her voice softening, "I am their light, their hope. A way out of their daily suffering."

But her tone turned icy when she talked about skeptics. "For those who deny me, I am the thing they fear most," she said flatly. "Mock me, and you will see what happens."

She told me belief and fear fed her. Every story, every ounce of doubt, every mocking laugh made her stronger. "I am born of reverence and ridicule," she said. "Every skeptic who denies me only adds to my power."

She made it clear why she'd chosen me. I was supposed to be her messenger, her voice in the world of the living. One minute she threatened me. The next she pleaded for my help. "Tell my story," she said. "Make them remember me, and I will offer you a warning, and maybe salvation."

I begged her to let me go, swearing I'd believe, that I'd tell people about her. She laughed, a sound so loud it made my ears hurt. Suddenly, I was back in my tent, drenched in sweat. But her laughter still echoed in my ears.

The next day, I felt different. All my usual pains, the constant headaches, the aches from years of drinking and drug use, the mental fog, they were gone. I felt lighter, healthier, like years of torment had just vanished. It was enough to make me seek out that group I'd mocked the day before.

They welcomed me back, no questions asked. They could see the change in me. As I listened to their stories, I realized they'd all had their own encounters with Candle Face. Each one was disturbing in its own way, and they had all chosen to believe. They'd become her disciples, spreading her story to keep others from facing her wrath.

I joined them. Night after night, we roamed the streets, sharing her story with anyone who'd listen. We thought we were doing the right thing, that maybe we could save others by spreading her message. Even as I told her story, I couldn't stop questioning it. Was Candle Face real? Or was she just a reflection of our fears? Something we'd created ourselves?

That doubt is what got me killed.

That night, she came to me again. In my dream, her face was even more grotesque than before. She leaned in close and hissed, "You lost faith."

Before I could speak, her hands were on me. Her charred fingers clamped down on my mouth and nose, cutting off my breath. Her skin was rough, like burnt wood, and the smell of scorched flesh filled the air.

I tried to fight, to scream, but she wouldn't let go. Her hollow eyes stared into mine with cruel satisfaction. Around us, shadows pulsed and shouted in a language I couldn't understand.

The edges of my vision started to fade, and my heart slowed. I realized too late that Candle Face was real, relentless, and unforgiving. My last thoughts were full of regret, knowing I'd made the mistake that got me killed: doubting her.

When everything went dark, I felt the cold sting of a needle in my arm, like she wanted me to remember the life I'd tried so hard to leave behind.

The Lost Soul stood up and walked toward the portal in the far corner of the room. His movements were slow, almost hesitant. As he neared it, his shadow stretched out behind him, and I noticed the needle still sticking out of his arm.

He paused at the portal's edge and looked back at me one last time. There was sadness in his eyes and a kind of acceptance. Then, without a word, he stepped through. The portal vanished, and the room was silent again, lit only by the soft glow from the kitchen light.

CANDLE FACE VICTIM #30: CANDLE FACE'S CONGREGATION

May 20, 2024

I finally put down my phone to prepare for another night on the couch. I walked to the light switch and turned it off. A much darker shadow appeared in the room's corner when the room went dark. I knew what was next, so I sat on the couch and waited. A short man wearing tattered clothing and a newer hoodie stepped out of the portal and approached me. I could smell his body odor when he became visible. We made eye contact, smiled, and he sat down beside me. He said good evening, then corrected himself with "Good mornin'," and laughed a little. He seemed so friendly I wanted to chat, but I knew better. After a short pause, he began his story:

I've heard folks say that a person's home is their sanctuary. Well, under the Ben White overpass, among the discarded and the lost, South Austin doesn't offer much of that. It's been a rough patch in life. Me and the other five had our own kind of brotherhood. We stuck together because we had to. What held us even tighter was fear, fear of something much worse than hunger, cold, or violence: Candle Face.

The stories of Candle Face were in every conversation around the fire pit. She was blamed for every misfortune, and people said those who doubted her existence ended up going mad, the kind of mad that lives in the bottom of bottles and at the tips of needles.

"Ever wonder why Kevin never came back?" Jim asked one night, his eyes haunted. "He doubted. Candle Face got him."

The group would nod along. They spoke of Candle Face. "We have to spread the word," they'd say. "We have to save the souls of the homeless."

I'd nod too, but my heart was never in it. To me, Candle Face was just a story, something born out of all the misery around us. I refused to believe in her powers. I needed a rational explanation for everything, for our fears and our horrors.

Then she came.

One night, a silhouette appeared by the fire, her eyes glowing like embers. The flames seemed to shrink in her presence, trembling as if they too feared her.

"One of you has betrayed me." Candle Face's voice was barely audible. Her gaze landed on me. I was the disbeliever, the one who pretended to go along while secretly doubting her.

She moved closer, and I felt the weight of her gaze strip away my pretense. She saw right through me. She didn't kill me. She turned to the others.

"This one shall be your warning," she said before vanishing into the burning fire pit.

My brothers, the ones I'd shared every hardship with, looked at me differently now. There was no warmth in their eyes anymore. Only fear and reverence. They believed I'd been marked, spared for a purpose.

Days passed, and the divide between us grew. They treated me like I was cursed, still alive, and tainted. Nights were worse. Shadows watched me from every corner, and the cold mocked our feeble fire. The others' belief in Candle Face deepened, and I became an outsider among them.

Then it came.

We gathered around the fire pit under the overpass. The flames danced wildly, their light casting jagged shadows on the concrete walls. This time, their eyes were hard. Set.

Candle Face appeared again, her flaming eyes fixed on us. She didn't speak. She didn't have to. The others rose, one by one. Their movements were slow and deliberate, their expressions unyielding. I knew what was coming.

They came at me with fists raised, like men carrying out an order. Every strike landed with purpose. Every blow was for Candle Face. Their grunts and gasps mixed with the crackling fire.

Pain exploded across my body, and I fell to the ground. They didn't stop. Each hit felt like punishment for my disbelief and for everything they had endured. Their anger, their misery, it all came down on me.

As my breath slowed and my vision dimmed, I saw her. Candle Face stood over us, watching in silence. Her eyes burned brighter, and for a moment, I thought I heard her voice.

"Believe," she said, the word sounding like an order.

And then everything went blank.

Personal Note to My Readers

For the first time in seven months of documenting the testimonies of the Lost Souls, names emerged. That is a real break in the pattern. Until now, these encounters were anonymous, their stories stripped of personal identifiers. The names Kevin and Jim change that. Jim was one of the victim's killers. That suggests a shift, or maybe a stronger need on the part of these spirits to be known and remembered.

As I write this journal entry, I want you to understand the significance of the moment. Kevin and Jim's names may mark the beginning of a new phase, where the Lost Souls start sharing more than their ghostly presence. Names bring histories and connections. With these first names, I expect more names and details to follow. That may become the new pattern as the spirits' stories grow less obscure.

CANDLE FACE VICTIM #31: CRYSTAL

May 24, 2024

I made a big mistake. I tried to sleep on the bed upstairs. This usually doesn't end well for me because sleeping flat, either on my stomach or back, brings on a major vertigo attack that will plague me for several days. That's what happened last night. Just as the room started to spin, the shadows stayed still. A woman stepped out of the shadowy portal and stood motionless while the rest of the room spun around her. She began her story as I tried to concentrate, knowing my vertigo attack would distract me from much of her testimony. Here's her story:

> I worked the corners of North Austin and, at times, downtown. I was a good prostitute. People would

ask for me by my street name, Crystal. I was also known to be rough and tough, and I wouldn't take crap from any man. Try to rip me off, and I'd punch, scratch, and kick until the son-of-a-bitch paid up.

One day, a man drove up and told me to get in. After a few minutes of dealing, I agreed, and we went to a secluded spot to seal the deal. He became a regular, maybe once every week, sometimes more often. He was quiet at first, but as we got more comfortable with each other, we would talk about life in general. He started talking about saving me and making me his wife. He wasn't the first person to say this. I knew that's when things started to get dangerous. I didn't want him to think I belonged to him, and I definitely didn't need a savior. But I needed the money, so I played along.

One day, he didn't want to pay me because he said I was his girl. When I mentioned that if he wanted to get laid, I needed to get paid, he hit me across the face. This wasn't the first time I got hit. I knew what to do. I bit him on his right cheek and punched him, and I got away. A few days later, he drove by and apologized, saying it was the drugs in his system that made him do it.

He looked at me with those puppy eyes, so I got into his truck. He drove me to our spot off the highway. I did my job, and he paid me. We continued this weekly for about two months. He pulled up next to me one day, and I got in. After doing the deed, we sat there talking like we used to. He brought up the story of Candle Face, the demon you named. He said he's a disciple of hers, responsible for spreading her word and bringing her anyone who doesn't believe in her. I asked what happens to those who don't believe. He said she'll deal with them individually. I just laughed, and eventually, we changed the subject. As the weeks passed, he wouldn't let it go. He kept asking me to help him spread the word about her and tell my friends about her. I would refuse, saying I just don't believe in ghosts.

One day, he asked me if I believed in Candle Face, and I went off on him. I got so tired of him asking me that I yelled at him and said no. I attempted to open the door, but he gripped my left arm and held me inside. I punched him with my right hand, but it barely landed. His punch to my face did land. He climbed on top of me and started to choke me, his thumbs pressed squarely into my neck. I knew this was going to be different from the other beatings I'd taken from my johns. I tried to scratch him, but couldn't reach his face. I tried to grab his hands and pry them off my neck, but it was no use. He was just too strong. Right before passing out, he stopped and laughed. He asked, "What's wrong? All the other girls like it." He then punched my face a few times and went back to choking me. This choking and punching pattern continued until I just couldn't fight or care anymore. He asked me, "Are you ready to believe?" I couldn't answer. My answer was still no. He went for my neck one final time, and death overtook me.

The second my life drained from my body, I appeared in a place filled with other souls. Shadows surrounded me, taller and skinnier than humans, gliding a foot or two above the ground. They grabbed me and told me that my job in death would be the same as in life: to entertain. I fell to my knees, which stuck to the ground. A shadow pushed me forward. My forearms hit the ground, and they, too, stuck to the ground. One of the shadows said, "Now that's the position you'll remain in for eternity." Other shadows formed two lines, one in front of me and the other behind me.

"Ray, I, um, I mean, we need your help. Please save us from this hell. You're the only one who can help us. You're paying too much attention to the wrong things."

I asked, "What can I do differently?" before realizing I had broken Candle Face's rule of not asking questions. I felt my heart sink, but she answered.

"Read and reread our testimonies. There are more clues in the testimonies. You must find them. You were chosen for a reason. All you have to do is…" she said in a rush, but a huge shadow figure appeared out of the portal. It had elongated limbs, and its eyes glowed a sickly red. The figure grabbed her by the neck with clawed hands, lifting her off the ground. She struggled, her form flickering and distorting.

The shadow looked at me and said in a voice that was both a whisper and a roar, "You were warned." Its breath was hot and foul, burning my skin and lungs. It then yanked her back through the portal with a force that made the air ripple and crack. As she was pulled through, her screams were sharp and piercing, echoing around me and mingling with the cries of other tormented souls. I was left alone, my mind racing with the message she left behind.

Personal Note to My Readers

As suspected, the Lost Souls are providing names now. This is the second Lost Soul who mentioned a name. This time, she mentioned her own street name, "Crystal." I realized that deciphering these hidden messages might be the key to their salvation. I need to review all the previous testimonies more thoroughly, searching for any clues Candle Face's victims left behind. This puzzle could be my path to freeing the tormented Lost Souls, including my own.

CANDLE FACE'S CODEX: THE LOST SOULS' SECRET MESSAGES

June 1, 2024

Just as Crystal told me last week, I need to pay more attention to the testimonies. So I applied Ramsey Theory to the spirits' testimonies and searched the text for hidden words and phrases.

Ramsey Theory is named after the British mathematician Frank P. Ramsey. It deals with the point at which order starts to appear inside what first looks random. It's usually discussed in mathematics and computer science, but the basic idea is familiar to intelligence work as well. When enough material is laid out in front of you, patterns start to show. One literary example appears in *Moby-Dick* by Herman Melville, published in 1851. By applying Ramsey Theory to *Moby-Dick*, researchers were able to identify hidden words and phrases tied to the novel's central concerns.

1. **"VENGEANCE"** The word "VENGEANCE" can be found hidden in the text, fitting Captain Ahab's relentless pursuit of the whale, Moby Dick. Ahab's drive for vengeance pushes the story forward and shows the destructive force of obsession. This hidden word points back to the novel's treatment of revenge and its consequences for Ahab and his crew.

2. **"MADNESS"** The word "MADNESS" is another hidden message found in *Moby Dick*. It points to the psychological unraveling of Captain Ahab and the crew during their voyage. Madness runs through the novel and tracks the line between sanity and insanity as Ahab's obsession with Moby Dick consumes him and affects the men around him.

These hidden words, found through the application of Ramsey Theory, align with the novel's central themes and character motives. They show how a long text can hold recurring patterns beneath its surface.

I used the same approach on *Candle Face Chronicles: The Lost Souls [Book One]*. I removed spaces, punctuation, and formatting from the text, then searched for words in multiple directions: up, down, backward, and diagonal. That search turned up a large number of words and phrases. Some appeared in every direction, which is why they drew my attention first. This journal entry examines the strongest of those words and phrases, what they may mean, and what they may suggest about the Lost Souls' testimonies.

Ramsey Theory Analysis

After removing spaces, punctuation, and formatting from *Candle Face Chronicles: The Lost Souls [Book One]* and searching for words up, down, backward, and diagonal, I found a large number of recurring words and phrases. Some stood out because they appeared in every direction, which may mean they matter more than the others. These words include "MAMA," "FIRE," "LOVE," "SAFE," "BURN," "SCARE," "NIGHT," "TIGHT," "GIRL," and "SAD." Each may point to something important in the Lost Souls' testimonies.

Analysis of Key Words and Phrases Found in All Directions:

1. **"MAMA"** Found 9 times in all directions, "MAMA" may point to the repeated presence of maternal figures in the testimonies. In "Candle Face Victim #2: Mama's Last Embrace," the young girl's testimony centers on her mother's protection and the separation that followed. This hidden word is more likely to refer to the young girl from the testimony of Tanisha Lorraine Watkins. Its repeated appearance may also matter for another reason. It raises the question of whether Candle Face's past involved a significant maternal bond that was damaged or broken.

2. **"FIRE"** Found 22 times in all directions, "FIRE" is tied directly to Candle Face's story and the trauma surrounding her. The fire on Ben Howell Drive in Austin, Texas, which claimed the life of a young boy and may have involved Candle Face herself, is a major event in my memoir *The Empty Lot Next Door*. The repeated appearance of "FIRE" suggests that this event sits close to the center of the spirits' stories and their

trauma. If that's true, then understanding what really happened in that fire may be necessary if I'm going to understand Candle Face or stop her.

3. "LOVE" Found 12 times in all directions, "LOVE" seems out of place at first in testimonies filled with fear and suffering. But the word may point to the bonds the spirits held onto in life. In "Mama's Last Embrace," the bond between the young girl and her mother stands in direct conflict with what Candle Face does. The repeated appearance of "LOVE" suggests that attachment, loyalty, and loss play a larger role in these testimonies than I first assumed.

4. "SAFE" Appearing 21 times in all directions, "SAFE" lines up with one of the clearest needs in these testimonies: the desire to be protected, sheltered, or left in peace. Many of the spirits speak as if safety was lost long before death. This word may point to a condition that has to be restored before the spirits can rest.

5. "BURN" Found 28 times in all directions, "BURN" is tied so directly to Candle Face that it's hard to separate it from her. The word points to literal burning and the lasting damage she leaves on people. Its repeated appearance may lead back to Candle Face's central trauma and to whatever keeps that trauma active.

6. "SCARE" Appearing 8 times in all directions, "SCARE" points to the role fear plays in how Candle Face controls her victims. The testimonies are filled with terror, and that fear is part of how she holds power over them. If that reading is correct, then fear may be part of the mechanism she uses.

7. **"NIGHT"** Found 8 times in all directions, "NIGHT" may refer to the time when Candle Face is most active and when the spirits come to me. The word may be practical as much as symbolic. Much of what I have learned from the Lost Souls has happened at night, which makes its repeated appearance hard to dismiss.

8. **"TIGHT"** Appearing 10 times in all directions, "TIGHT" may refer to physical restraint, emotional pressure, or the way fear closes in on the spirits. It may also point to the bonds between the spirits and the people they loved, bonds Candle Face seeks to destroy. This word suggests pressure, confinement, and attachment all at once.

9. **"GIRL"** Found 12 times in all directions, "GIRL" points back to Candle Face herself and to many of her victims, several of whom are young girls. The repeated appearance of this word stands out because so much of this case turns on girls, mothers, and the loss of safety at a young age. That pattern may hold clues to Candle Face's motives.

10. **"SAD"** Found 33 times in all directions, "SAD" captures the emotional tone that runs through nearly every testimony. Grief, loss, and longing sit at the center of these stories. The frequency of this word suggests that sorrow is built into the structure of the testimonies themselves.

Hidden Phrases in Spirit's Testimonies

Single words can point in a direction. Full phrases are harder to dismiss as chance and more likely to show intent. The following phrases were found using Ramsey Theory and may offer clearer clues than the single words alone:

1. **"ISAWMMAMA"** (direction = down) This appears to be a compressed version of "I SAW [MY] MAMA." It likely points to a memory tied to the little girl in "Mama's Last Embrace." It could mark a moment of comfort, trauma, or recognition. In a more disturbing reading, it could mean that her mother is also in Candle Face's Lair and that the little girl saw her there.

2. **"HOMEMOBILEROUS"** (direction = down) This phrase likely points to a mobile home, which aligns with the little girl's testimony in "Mama's Last Embrace" and her account of living in a mobile home with her mother and grandmother. Its appearance reinforces the setting of that testimony and the instability tied to it.

3. **"THEREMYGRANNY"** (direction = up) Translating to "THERE MY GRANNY," this phrase appears to point to the grandmother's presence and importance in the spirit's life. In "Mama's Last Embrace," Granny is a source of love and security. Another hard possibility is that her grandmother is also in Candle Face's Lair and that the little girl saw her there.

4. **"THEREMYGRANNYMA"** (direction = down) Similar to "THEREMYGRANNY," this phrase may read as "THERE MY GRANNY [AND MY] MA[MA]," again placing the grandmother and mother together. It may point to the combined importance of those maternal figures in the spirit's life. It could also mean that the little girl saw both of them in Candle Face's Lair.

5. "EYESLOVEONEMORE" (direction = diagonal upper right to bottom left) This phrase may point to a last look, a final plea, or the desire for one more moment of love and recognition. The wording is compressed, but the emotional direction is clear.

6. "SCAREREALTOUGHT" (direction = diagonal upper left to bottom right written backward) This phrase likely points to real fear. The spelling is rough, but the meaning appears clear enough. It reinforces the terror Candle Face instills in her victims and the fact that this fear feels immediate and physical.

7. "DONTPLEASEDONT" (direction = down) This phrase likely captures a direct plea. Of all the phrases found, this one is among the hardest to explain away. It sounds like a spirit begging for the pain to stop.

8. "TRELEE" (direction = up) This appears to be either an incomplete phrase or a name. A Google search shows that "TRELEE" is used as a first name. Without more context, I can't say more than that. It may still point to a specific spirit, person, or place.

9. "TEXAS" (direction = down) The appearance of "TEXAS" confirms the geographical setting of all of the spirits' testimonies. So far, every story points back to Texas, especially Austin, and this phrase reinforces the importance of location in the larger pattern.

Analysis of Hidden Phrases

The hidden phrases found in *Candle Face Chronicles: The Lost Souls*

[Book One] point most clearly in four directions:

- **Familial Connections:** Phrases like "ISAWMMAMA," "THEREMYGRANNY," and "THEREMYGRANNYMA" point back to mothers and grandmothers, especially in "Mama's Last Embrace." If that reading is correct, then the female family line in that testimony plays a larger role than I first realized.
- **Settings and Context:** "HOMEMOBILEROUS" and "TEXAS" provide details about the settings of the spirits' lives and deaths. The reference to a mobile home fits the testimony connected to Tanisha Lorraine Watkins and grounds that story in a specific place and living situation. "TEXAS" places the broader pattern inside a clear regional setting.
- **Emotional States:** Phrases like "EYESLOVEONEMORE," "SCAREREALTOUGHT," and "DONTPLEASEDONT" point to longing, fear, and desperation. These emotions run through the testimonies and shape the spirits' experience.
- **Desperation and Fear:** The repeated pleading and fear, especially in "SCAREREALTOUGHT" and "DONTPLEASEDONT," show the helplessness the Lost Souls carry. These phrases point to sustained psychological torment.

Taken together, these phrases suggest that the testimonies contain a second layer of information. They point to identity, relationships, memory, and emotional condition. They may also point to ways of understanding Candle Face's hold on the spirits and, possibly, ways of weakening it.

Interpretation of the Hidden Messages

The words found in all directions in *Candle Face Chronicles: The Lost Souls [Book One]* appear to point toward two connected issues: Candle Face's identity and the conditions that might weaken her power. Maternal ties ("MAMA"), fire ("FIRE"), and the repeated need for safety and love ("SAFE," "LOVE") keep pulling me back to Candle Face's past, especially her relationship with her mother and the events of the fire. Fear ("SCARE"), sadness ("SAD"), and night ("NIGHT") point to the conditions in which she operates and the emotional state she creates.

The repeated appearance of "GIRL" is also important. It points back to Candle Face and to many of her victims, several of whom are young girls. That pattern could help explain her motives and choice of victims.

If these patterns are real, then the testimonies may be pointing toward more than memory. The unresolved grief, fear, and attachment running through them may be tied to how Candle Face keeps these souls trapped in her Lair.

The application of Ramsey Theory to *Candle Face Chronicles: The Lost Souls [Book One]* exposed a set of recurring words and phrases that I can't ignore. Each one needs more work. I need to test them again, compare them across testimonies, and see whether the same patterns hold as new spirits come forward.

If any of my readers have ideas about the meaning of these hidden messages, please contact me. The words suggest a path toward understanding Candle Face's past and finding a way to help the Lost

Souls.

Here's a list of additional words that were found written backward in all directions, listed in order of appearance:

ETAH - HATE
EFIL - LIFE
ELPOEP - PEOPLE
GNINNIGEB - BEGINNING
STNERAP - PARENTS
SDNEIRF - FRIENDS
TNAW - WANT
DLROW - WORLD
DEVIVRUS - SURVIVED
NEVAEH - HEAVEN
LLEH - HELL
DEPPANDIK - KIDNAPPED
DEPOH - HOPED
EKAW - WAKE
DEIRC - CRIED
HTAED - DEATH
YDOB - BODY
YARTEB - BETRAY
SLLIK - KILLS
DAED - DEAD
PLEH - HELP
ESAELP - PLEASE
EID - DIE

CANDLE FACE VICTIM #32: CLEAN SHAVEN

June 5, 2024

The lights started to flicker shortly after midnight, more than they had in the last few days. I thought nothing of it, so I continued my nightly scrolling through YouTube videos. When one of the flickers lasted long enough to disconnect the internet, I looked up and saw a woman with what appeared to be a broken jaw, blood covering her face and dripping down between her legs. I put down my phone. This time, I didn't motion for her to sit next to me. I just sat there and waited for her to begin. I smiled, and she returned it. A few teeth fell out, which she quickly picked up and put back in her mouth. She began her story, speaking slowly, knowing it would be hard for me to understand. Here's her story:

Hi Ray, my name is Cayman. I loved and hated my husband. Our relationship was lovey-dovey one minute and conflict the next. Our arguments were mostly about money and his wandering eye, especially his obsession with young girls. He had a thing for young girls, and I tried to look younger by shaving down there. He liked it at first. Soon enough, he wanted the real thing.

On the day I died, we fought over something trivial, though I can't recall exactly what because we were both drunk and looking for a fight. I got right up in his face and spat at him. Enraged, he punched me in the face, and I hit the edge of the end table. He climbed on top of me and started hitting me in the mouth, warning me that if I ever spat on him again, he'd kill me. When he finally stopped, my mouth and my left cheekbone felt like mush. He seemed to realize he had gone too far and panicked. I was barely conscious as he yelled, "Look what you made me do!" All I could see were his feet pacing back and forth.

He lifted me into a sitting position against the couch. My eyes were barely open as he looked at me and said, "I'm sorry." I spat in his face again, blood and snot mixing in the spit that landed mostly in his mouth. Furious, he threw me back to the floor and stomped on my head and neck until I was no more. The whole time, I was laughing at the futility of it all.

When I died, I stared at the most wicked figure I had ever seen. It had the form of a woman with long hair, and her eyes were empty and seemed to pierce into my soul. She welcomed me to her Lair, saying I'd find my place there, though I had arrived early. She explained that my husband had killed me too soon. I was meant to be sacrificed later because of my disbelief. I tried to speak, but my mouth was full of broken teeth and blood. She then pronounced my eternal punishment: for the rest of eternity, a razor would keep me clean shaven for the shadows to enjoy.

She gave me a half-smile while holding her hands just below her mouth, maybe to catch her teeth if they fell out again. She turned and walked slowly toward the shadowy portal. One step before reaching it, she hesitated and began to cry. A loud and thunderous voice rang out, "Come." She stepped into the portal and disappeared.

Personal Note to My Readers

Another Lost Soul provided me with a name: Cayman, or Caymen. It could also be Clayman or Claymen, as it was difficult to understand her through the gargling and broken teeth. Her voice was distorted and echoed unnaturally, causing me to miss every third or fourth word. I did a Google search for any missing persons with that first, middle, or last name who might have gone missing in Central Texas. I haven't found any leads yet, but I'll continue looking.

CANDLE FACE VICTIMS #33 AND #34: DROWNED DREAMS

June 7, 2024

I slept early last night. Just as I hit the pillow, the shadows in the living room corner began to flicker, along with the kitchen lights I left on to help cast a shadow in that corner. I sat up and saw two figures exit the portal and walk toward me. As they neared, I saw that one was a white man around 60. He was rather short, standing around 5'8" or so. The other Lost Soul was a much younger woman, maybe 25 or younger. She appeared black or light-skinned Hispanic, but I couldn't tell for sure.

The male spirit spoke first.

"Hello, Ray. Moana and I need your help."

Moana looked puzzled. "What did you say?"

Standing to her left, the male spirit switched sides with Moana and nearly yelled in her right ear, "I told Ray we need his help."

"Oh yes, Ray, we need your help," she repeated.

We just looked at each other, waiting for the other to respond. I wanted to ask them how to help, but I knew better than to ask.

After looking around confused, Moana spoke. "Ray, we drowned in Lake Travis around 20 years ago. We both had dreams of Candle Face the night before. Even though we weren't together that night, we had the same dream from our own perspectives."

The male spirit nodded. "I always believed in Candle Face, but I didn't want to follow her directions, like bringing non-believers to her. I drew the line at taking part in killings."

"Me too, I didn't want any part of that," Moana added.

"In my dream, Candle Face said if I didn't listen to her, I'd be her next victim," the male spirit continued. "Moana had the same dream."

The male spirit paused, then added, "Candle Face chooses her followers carefully. She targets those who already believe in her but are weak enough to manipulate. She preys on our fears and desires, making promises and threats in our dreams. We were chosen because we both had a history of dabbling in the paranormal. She used our curiosity and fear against us."

Moana nodded in agreement. "She promised us power and knowledge beyond the grave if we brought non-believers to her. It seemed harmless enough at first, just convincing people to believe in Candle Face's power. Then she demanded more. She wanted us to lead people to their deaths, to feed her power."

"We couldn't do it," the male spirit said, his voice shaking. "We refused to become murderers. Defying her came with a price."

"Soon after we got in the middle of the lake that day, the boat nearly tipped over, and we both fell overboard. Moana didn't know how to swim, so she went underwater. I dived down after her. Once I was underwater, I could see about a dozen skeletal figures grabbing her legs and pulling her down toward the bottom. I tried to pull her back up."

Moana continued, "But the monsters were just too strong. They kept pulling me down to the bottom. I was almost out of air by then, but I saw a few more monsters on the bottom, holding up a large rock. I was placed at the bottom, and the rock was placed on top of me, finishing the job."

The male spirit said, "I was almost out of air, too, but I continued to swim down after her. When the rock was in place, the group came after me. They, too, put me under a large rock. Our bodies are still under those rocks, near the marina where we launched the boat."

"Ray, help free us from the rocks," Moana pleaded. "If you can find our bodies, our souls will also be free from Candle Face. Please help us."

The two spirits thanked me and walked back toward the portal. The male whispered something in Moana's right ear, but I couldn't hear it. They both stepped in and disappeared.

Personal Note to My Readers

During my high school years, I visited this general area often. I would jump off the cliffs at Pale Face and relax in the water at The Flats. I enjoyed my time there with my friends. Many people have drowned in those waters, and many of their bodies were never recovered. It's possible some of those who never resurfaced could be the "monsters" pulling down Moana and her male companion.

In December 2023, a Candle Face victim visited me to tell me his testimony. I kept putting off writing his story in my online journal. On February 13, 2024, he revisited me, hit me a few times, and even vomited in my mouth. He warned me not to ignore any more spirits. This spirit also drowned in Lake Travis while he was on an overnight boat trip with his two young sons.

Recently, a pattern started to stand out. Three spirits in a row who visited me were all victims of drowning, killed by Candle Face. That pushes me to investigate more deeply and understand what connects these testimonies.

I think there have been four drowning victims so far, and there are likely many more. There have been a lot of bodies found in Town

Lake, or what the new generation of Austinites call Lady Bird Lake. Many believe there's a serial killer on the loose.

A few months ago, I began my investigation. The stories of these Lost Souls, each ending in water, point to a horrifying possibility: Candle Face is the serial killer responsible for the drowning deaths in Austin and nearby Lake Travis.

Despite the police's best efforts, the cases remain unsolved. The only link is the victims' supposed interactions with Candle Face. One of my visiting spirits thought he was helping a drowning child, only to be pulled under the surface by Candle Face.

Water appears to play a significant role in Candle Face's killings. Several of her victims are associated with bodies of water, and she often appears near lakes, rivers, and the creek near my childhood home. There are several possible reasons water is so central to her actions:

1. **Elemental Connection:** Candle Face may have an elemental connection to water, using it as a conduit for her power. Water might amplify her abilities, allowing her to manipulate and kill her victims more easily.

2. **Portal to the Underworld:** In some cultures, like the Mayans, bodies of water serve as portals to the underworld. Through these portals, she can drag her victims into her Lair.

3. **Manifestation of Fear:** Water may bring out the deepest fears of her victims. Many people have a primal fear of drowning, and Candle Face uses that fear to control and terrorize her targets.

To understand Candle Face, on 30 October 2023, I interviewed an 82-year-old gentleman who claimed to have seen her. Around 1990, while walking his dog near the creek at the intersection of Wilson and

El Paso Streets in Austin, TX, he saw a young girl with long dark hair seemingly bathing in the water. They locked eyes, and he thought he heard a voice asking, "Do you believe?" He whispered, "Yes." He never saw her again, but he knew it was Candle Face.

Mr. Doe's story, along with the spirits' testimonies and the serial killer rumors, suggests Candle Face may be a vengeful ghost or a manifestation of the city's fears. As their confidant, I find myself trying to solve the case behind the serial killer rumors haunting Austin.

The task is difficult. It has to be done. By piecing together the personal tragedies of the spirits with the fear hanging over Austin, I hope to better understand what's happening in the waters of Town Lake, Lake Travis, and everywhere else Candle Face's presence remains.

IDENTIFIED? – CANDLE FACE VICTIM #25 AND #26: THE PEN PAL LETTERS

June 9, 2024

On June 4, 2024, a commenter responded to the April 17, 2024, Candle Face Victim #25 and #26: The Pen Pal Letters journal entry. The commenter believes one of the victims described in the journal entry is her friend, Sonya Wallace, who was killed in February 1999. Here's her comment:

> A friend of mine sent me this article of yours. She said it sounded a lot like our friend Sonya Wallace. Sonya was last seen leaving a post office in Rockdale on February 19, 1999. She said she had to drop off a letter at the post office. No one knows who she was mailing a letter to. The news said her head

was smashed in. Maybe this is farfetched, but if it was Sonya who visited you, please help her. Please find a way to help her escape Candle Face. If you have any questions, please email.

Could the spirit who visited me on April 17, 2024, have been Sonya Wallace? After researching her name, I found dozens of news reports about her disappearance and the discovery of her remains. Those reports go back more than two and a half decades.

According to a CBS Austin article, Sonya Wallace was a 15-year-old from Rockdale, Texas, about 60 miles east of Austin. She disappeared on February 19, 1999, while walking from the post office, and her body was found three weeks later in a creek bed in east Williamson County. At the time, she was a student at Rockdale High School and had connections in Rockdale, Taylor, Elgin, and Austin.

Read the CBS Austin article here: https://cbsaustin.com/news/local/williamson-county-sheriffs-office-asking-for-help-in-1999-cold-case-sonya-wallace-rockdale-taylor-elgin-austin-disappearance-teenager-death

The spirit's April 17, 2024, testimony describes her encounter with Candle Face. She also mentions a series of exchanges with her pen pal from San Francisco, which turn dark when the pen pal becomes obsessed with the legend of Candle Face.

The Lost Soul says her pen pal's letters grew more frantic and full of fear. The pen pal disappears, and the Lost Soul later encounters Candle Face, leading to her death from a blow to the head with a large rock.

Here are some similarities between the spirit's testimony and news reports about Sonya Wallace:

- **Disappearance and Discovery:** Sonya Wallace disappeared while walking from the post office, and her body was found weeks later. The spirit's testimony also mentions walking from the post office and disappearing afterward.

- **Geographic Connection:** Sonya Wallace had connections in Rockdale, Taylor, Elgin, and Austin, which fits the Lost Soul's description of moving through these areas and their connection to Candle Face, which is centered in the Austin area.

- **Paranormal Elements:** The involvement of Candle Face in the spirit's testimony lines up with the unexplained nature of Sonya Wallace's disappearance and death and suggests a paranormal cause.

- **Cause of Death:** Both Sonya Wallace and the Lost Soul were killed by blows to the head. According to news reports, Sonya Wallace's head was bludgeoned, while the Lost Soul's testimony describes a large rock being used to kill her.

Possible Contrasts

- **Pen Pal's Location:** The Lost Soul's testimony mentions a pen pal from San Francisco, which doesn't match Sonya Wallace's known connections.

- **Age Difference:** Sonya Wallace was a 15-year-old high school student at the time of her disappearance. The spirit who visited me was much older than 15, likely in her mid-twenties.

- **Timeline and Additional Missing Persons:** The spirit's testimony doesn't specify a timeline for the pen pal's disappearance. Further investigation is needed to determine whether a girl from San Francisco went missing from late January to mid-February 1999, which could provide more context.
- **Communication Methods:** The spirit's testimony says she and her pen pal communicated by letters. Facebook and other social media had no place in that account. This stands out because Facebook went live to the general public in September 2006, more than six years after Sonya Wallace went missing. That raises the possibility that the spirit was someone else who died in a similar way after Facebook became widely used.

Based on the similarities in background, geographic connection, and the circumstances of the disappearance, it's possible that Sonya Wallace was the Lost Soul from Candle Face Victim #25 and #26: The Pen Pal Letters. The age difference and the communication details in the spirit's testimony also leave open the possibility that this was someone else who died in a similar way after 2006.

Further Investigation

Further investigation into the connection between the real-life case of Sonya Wallace and the spirit's testimony is needed. This could involve:

- Investigating whether a girl from San Francisco went missing from late January to mid-February 1999. This could provide more context and possible connections.

- Investigating other potential victims in Central Texas who disappeared in a similar way after 2006, when Facebook became widely used.

JOIN ME ON PARANORMALLYBLONDE TO TALK ABOUT CANDLE FACE

June 10, 2024

https://www.youtube.com/live/pMNZCEaApB0

Join me to talk about Candle Face Chronicles, a two-part series that examines Candle Face and the case growing around her. The series includes *The Lost Souls* and *Genesis* and invites readers to work with me, a retired intelligence analyst and private investigator with more than thirty years of experience.

Candle Face Chronicles: The Lost Souls is a collection of testimonies and an investigation into real-life encounters with spirits who were victims of Candle Face. As skeptics turned victims share their testimonies, readers are asked to help bring peace to these Lost Souls.

That work includes locating spirits' remains, identifying their killers, piecing together testimonies, analyzing cryptic messages, researching historical records, and sorting through the visions these spirits communicate. Both parts of the Chronicles use technology alongside traditional and unconventional investigative techniques. Participants can also share findings and theories through an interactive website and podcast.

In *Candle Face Chronicles: Genesis*, the investigation turns more directly to Candle Face herself. It follows visits to haunted sites and discussions with people in paranormal research, theology, and demonology in an effort to understand what she is. Who's Candle Face? A fallen angel, a demon, or an entirely unknown type of entity?

The *Candle Face Chronicles* centers on collaborative investigation and reader participation as part of the effort to solve cold cases. Participants are encouraged to share their analysis and add to the investigation.

If you read the books or take part in the investigation, you become part of the effort to seek justice and peace for the spirits harmed by Candle Face.

Join me as I discuss *Candle Face Chronicles: The Lost Souls* and *Genesis*. Whether Candle Face is a ghost, a fallen angel, a demon, or something else entirely, each testimony and clue will help this investigation.

PSYCHIC SPIES AND LOST SOULS

June 14, 2024

During my June 10, 2024, podcast on PARANORMALLYblonde with Robert Stachowicz and Sara Jane Kamyszek Villani, a viewer suggested I learn remote viewing to help the Lost Souls. The viewer, Stacey Tallitsch, says he's a professional remote viewer. Tallitsch says he trained for 15 years under Major Ed Dames, who led the United States Military's "Psychic Spy" program, the Stargate Project, later known as the "Icarus Project" under the FBI.

Tallitsch now works with retired FBI agents in the FindMe group to locate missing children. He has also applied his skills to the stock market for Fortune 500 companies and to disaster remediation for man-made catastrophes. Tallitsch says he accurately predicted election outcomes, the rise of Pope Francis, various sporting events, and the

Arab Spring.

Tallitsch now teaches basic and advanced topics in remote viewing on Udemy, an educational platform with over 75,000 instructors and 64 million students covering more than 210,000 courses.

Read about Tallitsch's remote classes here: www.udemy.com/user/staceytallitsch

According to the course description, remote viewing was developed by the United States military to "turn regular 'off the street' people how [sic] to become psychic spies." Tallitsch's classes teach students to distinguish intuitive information from imagination and to target and gather information on a person, place, thing, or event anywhere in space and time.

Is remote viewing real? The U.S. military apparently thought it was real enough to create a program called the Stargate Project. It was a secret U.S. Army unit established in 1978 at Fort Meade, Maryland, by the Defense Intelligence Agency (DIA) and SRI International, a California contractor. The program investigated the potential use of psychic phenomena in military and domestic intelligence applications.

The program was initiated in response to Soviet research on psychic phenomena as part of the Cold War intelligence race. The Stargate Project and its related programs were eventually declassified and terminated in 1995 after the intelligence community concluded the methods didn't provide actionable intelligence.

Remote viewing involves entering a meditative state, clearing the mind of distractions, and focusing on the target: a person, location, or event. The information gained from remote viewing sessions could then be cross-referenced with known facts to test its accuracy and provide possible leads.

Remote viewing could help the Lost Souls who visit me at night. These souls, victims of Candle Face or her followers, come to me seeking help to find their bodies and identify their killers. By using remote viewing techniques, I could potentially gather intuitive information about the locations of their remains and the circumstances of their deaths, including who killed them. This process involves targeting specific information across space and time so I can perceive details that would otherwise stay hidden. By developing this skill, I hope to give these Lost Souls some closure and bring justice to their cases.

Do I believe in remote viewing? No, I don't. Still, I didn't think a person could control dreams either. But when I learned to control my dreams as a child, I used that ability to fight Candle Face and [temporarily] beat her. So I won't dismiss remote viewing just yet. I'll take Tallitsch's courses and keep an open mind. I'll do anything to help the Lost Souls.

COMING SOON: CANDLE FACE CHRONICLES PODCAST

June 19, 2024

The upcoming Candle Face Chronicles Podcast will explore the testimonies of Candle Face's victims. Our mission is to help locate their remains and identify their killers. A key part of the podcast is the "Advisory Board," made up of volunteers from different paranormal and investigative backgrounds. This group includes paranormal investigators, psychics, mediums, criminal investigators, and people with little paranormal experience to help keep the viewpoints balanced. Each board member brings something different to the cases we examine.

This podcast is a collaborative effort. No one can do this alone, and we value your input. We hold our sessions every Thursday at 8:00

p.m. CST, starting June 20th. The day before, I brief the board on the topic through the Candle Face website, usually focusing on specific victims, so they can come prepared. Each podcast is limited to one hour. That helps us stay focused and keep the discussion concise. During each podcast, board members have a chance to introduce themselves and explain their background. I present a detailed account of that day's cases, likely covering two victims, and share relevant clues. Board members then offer their analysis, readings, or other information to help solve these cases. We also count on our listeners to contribute additional information and analysis about the victims' stories. Your contribution may help solve these cases and bring peace to those Lost Souls.

We're doing this because we want to help bring resolution to Candle Face's victims. With three decades of experience in intelligence analysis and as a missing persons and human trafficking investigator, I'm now applying those skills to this spiritual effort. We hope to free these spirits from Candle Face's Lair. We're committed to pooling our skills and knowledge to help these Lost Souls.

I originally reached out to the public for help through my online journal. That approach has been effective and may have helped identify five of the 34 Lost Souls. I believe a podcast may work even better because it allows me to share my screen and show possible evidence such as maps, photographs, and historical documents. The live format also makes it easier to get real-time input and discussion, which could help us solve these cases.

If you have any questions or would like to discuss this further, please contact me through Facebook Messenger.

CANDLE FACE CHRONICLES PODCAST: THE FIRST EPISODE

June 20, 2024

https://youtu.be/zEfnItuwtL8

Join me, Arthur Mills, along with special guests Robert Stachowicz and Sara Jane Kamyszek Villani from the Get Haunted Network, as we launch the Candle Face Chronicles Podcast. We hope this podcast will help bring peace to the Lost Souls by locating their remains and identifying their killers.

CANDLE FACE CHRONICLES: THE PODCAST BEGINS

June 21, 2024

Yesterday marked an important step for me as I launched the first episode of my podcast, Candle Face Chronicles Podcast, on June 20, 2024. Getting into podcasting was exciting and nerve-wracking, and it wouldn't have been possible without the support of Robert Stachowicz and Sara Jane Kamyszek Villani from Get Haunted.

My first attempt at podcasting was almost a disaster. I hadn't lined up any guests until the night before the show, and that planning mistake left me scrambling. Rob and Sara stepped up and made sure the show still happened. Despite my late arrival at my own show and technical glitches caused by "Gremlins" that repeatedly froze my image, they kept the conversation going and the audience engaged while I figured out how to join my own show.

After the technical difficulties, I finally managed to join the podcast using my smartphone. I might not have made the best first impression. I was still eager to get into the main subject. We discussed Candle Face, her victims known as the Lost Souls, and the origins tied to *The Empty Lot Next Door.*

The podcast centers on collaboration and investigation. Each episode is a group effort with the goal of helping the Lost Souls find peace. This project is supported by the "Dream Team," made up of volunteers from different backgrounds, including paranormal investigators, psychics, mediums, remote viewers, dream interpreters, and people with very little paranormal experience. Their different viewpoints help us look at each case from more than one angle.

As the two-hour debut episode wrapped up, the feedback was very positive. I still have a lot of room for improvement, and the podcast clearly has the potential to be useful and to offer hope to those affected by Candle Face.

Looking ahead, I'm eager to continue this project with the "Dream Team." Together, we'll work to help the Lost Souls find their bodies and identify their killers. Each week, the Dream Team members and I will investigate specific cases, present evidence, share our analysis, and invite viewers to contribute.

The first episode of Candle Face Chronicles wasn't perfect. Far from it. It taught me a lot and got this project moving. I'm grateful for your support and look forward to your continued involvement.

CANDLE FACE CHRONICLES PODCAST: VICTIM #3

June 27, 2024

https://youtu.be/HrMWNvrJH5Q

On Nov. 23, 2023, I was visited by two Lost Souls, a man and a woman. They asked for my help, told me how they were brutally killed by someone they once trusted, and wanted me to tell the truth and identify their killer.

CANDLE FACE VICTIM #35: THE LURE OF LULING

June 30, 2024

It's been three weeks since the last Lost Soul visited me. This isn't the first time there's been a long pause, so I knew they'd eventually return. Last night, they did. I was preparing the couch as my makeshift bed when the lights began to flicker, and the shadows in the corner of the living room formed into the familiar portal.

Out stepped a man who walked straight toward me like he owned the place. During a podcast two days ago with Stacey Tallitsch, he suggested I pay close attention to the details of the spirits who visit me. Although I had tried this before with little success, I had better luck this time. I looked him over, hoping to catch details about his appearance. He was a white male in his mid-twenties with long, unkempt, dirty blond hair, wearing a dark T-shirt with a single word above an indistinct image. Despite my efforts, I couldn't make out what it said, and I felt awkward staring at his T-shirt, much like trying to read a woman's T-shirt without looking like a creep. He sat beside me, his body facing the portal, but his head turned toward me. I nodded, and he began his testimony.

Ray, my name is Dave, and I'm here to tell you my story. In October 2000, I went to a concert where I met a few friends. They were metalheads like me, into bands like Metallica, Slayer, and Pantera. We started hanging out and dreaming of starting our own heavy metal band.

One day, our drummer mentioned writing a song that would brainwash fans into becoming fiercely loyal, even to the point of carrying out Candle Face's wishes. He explained how we could embed subliminal messages within the aggressive beats, using layered vocals and reversed audio tracks. These messages would influence listeners to buy our CDs and follow Candle Face's orders. The focus of our lyrics would be on Candle Face, pulling in others who shared our musical taste and turning them into her instruments.

The drummer was deeply involved in the occult and believed in Candle Face, the ghost that haunts and kills those who don't believe in her. He saw our music as a way to spread her word, convincing followers to spread her power. Each song would contain hidden messages, encouraging loyalty and promoting her evil agenda. The music was a twisted form of worship meant to enthrall our listeners and spread her word.

At first, I was all in. We wrote our first song about an evil spirit demanding loyalty from its followers. The first few lines went something like this: "In darkness, we kneel, our goddess reigns, heed her call, forsake your chains!" We created a second song that was even more disturbing, demanding that our fans destroy and kill for her. Both songs were supposed to have reversed tracks that would list the names of people to kill, and the drummer would provide the names.

As we perfected our new songs, I heard voices in my head. These voices demanded my genuine participation, claiming the subliminal messages would be hidden in my guitar playing. I took part, but my heart wasn't in it. The voices grew louder and more intense, accusing me of being a traitor to Candle Face and my bandmates. Desperate to repel the voices, I branded a cross on my left arm, thinking it would protect me. I had first considered branding it on my forehead, but that would draw too much attention.

One day, my bandmates came to my house with the CD of our two songs. The drummer suggested we go to the woods to play the music undisturbed through his loud car stereo. We all jumped into his car and drove south on 183, way outside Austin. We came to a mostly dirt road and parked. We all got out of the car, and the drummer turned on the first song at full blast. We all sang along and air-played our instruments as if we were in a major rock concert at the Frank Erwin Center.

When the songs were over, the drummer asked me what I thought. I told him they were our best yet. Then he played the second song in reverse, and the hidden message said: "In the name of our Mother, spill the blood. Nonbelievers must now fall, heed her call, one and all." He played more of the second song in reverse, revealing a list of names for their followers to kill. On the list was the name "Dave."

As the reversed track played and my name came up, I laughed nervously, hoping it was just a sick joke or coincidence. After all, I'm not the only Dave out there. But my bandmates turned on me, showing they knew I wasn't a true believer in Candle Face. They beat me, leaving me barely conscious. They took me to a nearby abandoned house where Candle Face awaited. Confused and desperate, I asked why this was happening to me. I was a band member. Furious, Candle Face explained that true dedication was required, and I failed by not genuinely believing in the music's power.

In a final twist, Candle Face mocked me for believing a cross on my arm could repel her. She said, "You think that cross could protect you? I will place you under the floorboards with others who thought they could beat me." Beneath the floorboards lay the souls of those who had also faltered in their loyalty, their screams heard

> through the house: "Half-hearted devotion leads
> to eternal derision."

When he was done, he stood up and said, "Ray, it's better to believe, just in case." He briskly walked back to the portal and stepped in. This is the second time I have heard this phrase.

Personal Note to My Readers

I believe the house mentioned by Dave may be the same one referenced by Victims #24 and #27. In all three cases, Candle Face places her victims under the floorboards. Could this be the same house in Luling, TX? Dave mentioned that he and his bandmates drove south on 183 and stopped on a mostly dirt road, likely Salt Flat Road. Could this be the same road and house?

As I write this, I feel a strong pull toward the house, like I'm hypnotized. It's as if invisible forces are pushing me to go, the urge becoming almost irresistible. Deafening screams fill my head, echoing with urgency and telling me to get there now. The compulsion is so intense that it drowns out all rational thought. It's 3:30 in the morning, and I can make it to Luling in about two hours. The idea of confronting whatever lies there terrifies me and pulls me in at the same time. I headed out the door and began my journey.

Update

About an hour from Luling, I called my friend Michael, "Mark" in my memoir *The Empty Lot Next Door*. He's a night owl, so I knew he would be awake. I thought that if he left now, we could both reach the house at the same time. However, Michael frantically begged me not to go, warning me about the dangers of confronting whatever presence might be there. He reminded me of the threatening stories surrounding Candle Face and that house, insisting that going alone, or even with him, was dangerous. He urged me to turn around and go back home. I listened to Michael and turned around. After talking to him, the eagerness faded.

I can't help but wonder if this was a trap. Was it Candle Face's way of luring me in and finally ending my investigation and my life once and for all? Am I digging too deep into Candle Face? What would have happened if I had actually reached the house? Would I have ended up under the floorboards, just another victim added to her collection? What if I had arrived alone, or worse, taken Michael with me? The danger we might have faced is hard to ignore. It leaves me wondering how far I'm willing to go in this pursuit and whether some mysteries are better left unsolved.

Where do I go from here? Is it really up to me? These questions are pulling me in different directions. Should I continue investigating Candle Face, or is it wiser to walk away while I still can? But I still have to help the Lost Souls. Then again, why would Candle Face insist that I help them and set a trap for me at the same time? I just don't get it. What games is she playing?

CANDLE FACE CHRONICLES PODCAST: IS THE MYSTERY VISITOR TANISHA'S SPIRIT?

July 3, 2024

https://youtu.be/ERguUgIJcqY

Stacey Tallitsch and I discuss the case of a missing young girl whose spirit may still be seeking justice. Could the spirit who visited me on November 18, 2023, have been Tanisha, the girl who vanished from her swing set in front of her mobile home?

DISTINGUISHING REALITY FROM IMAGINATION: THE CANDLE FACE DEBATE (PART 1)

July 5, 2024

SPOILER ALERT: This journal entry contains information about characters and themes in *The Empty Lot Next Door*. If you want to avoid spoilers, stop here until you've finished the book. Reading this journal entry may give away plot details you may prefer to discover on your own.

This is the first entry in a two-part series on the legend of Candle Face, an evil entity that haunted my childhood. In this entry, I examine the possibility that Candle Face was a manifestation of past trauma rooted in my own mind. In the second entry, I examine the possibility that Candle Face is a real ghostly presence, separate from my own psyche.

As you read these two accounts, weigh the evidence and decide for yourself whether Candle Face is a supernatural entity or a manifestation of my past trauma.

Candle Face has been a constant presence from my earliest memories, tied to my deepest fears and anxieties. As I've grown and reflected on those years, I've started to believe Candle Face was a creation of my own imagination, a manifestation of the inner turmoil and emotional upheaval I experienced as a child.

My childhood was marked by challenging circumstances, including family tensions, social isolation, and a constant sense of being different from my peers. In that context, Candle Face became a tangible symbol of fears and anxieties I couldn't articulate or understand at the time. She was a projection of the turmoil within me, a way for my young mind to cope with and externalize emotional chaos I was unable to process.

The details and consistency of Candle Face's appearances, which some may see as evidence of her reality, can also be read as the work of a highly imaginative and sensitive child's mind. Children, especially those facing emotional stress, often create detailed and consistent imaginary worlds, as my brother Ricky did with the stories he shared with the neighborhood kids at his treehouse. Those worlds provide a safe space to explore and process complex emotions and experiences. The vividness of Candle Face's presence, her actions, and the terror she caused reflected the depth of my internal struggles.

The physical manifestations attributed to Candle Face, the scratches and disturbances in my room, can be understood as psychosomatic responses. The human mind can produce physical symptoms in response to psychological stress. In times of intense fear or anxiety, the body can react in ways that mimic physical harm caused by an external source.

My shared experiences with Ricky, often cited as proof of Candle Face, can be explained through shared delusions, or folie à deux. This psychological condition occurs when one person's delusional beliefs are transmitted to another, especially in close relationships. Our bond, combined with the power of suggestion and the heightened emotional state we were in, could have led to shared hallucinations of Candle Face.

As for the emotional and psychological impact of these encounters, it's undeniable. The depth of that impact alone can't settle whether Candle Face was real. Mental creations can affect us deeply, especially when they grow out of deep-seated fears and unresolved trauma.

The specific knowledge and foresight attributed to Candle Face could have come from my subconscious mind processing observations and information that my conscious mind hadn't fully acknowledged. Children are often more perceptive than they're given credit for, and it's possible that I picked up on cues and details about my environment and future events without fully realizing it.

The apparent purpose behind Candle Face's actions could reflect my need for structure and understanding in a chaotic and unpredictable world. By giving those qualities to an imaginary figure, I was trying to make sense of what felt senseless and find meaning in the randomness of life.

The nature of Candle Face's appearances, tied to specific emotional states or events, also fits the theory that she was a product of my imagination. Our fears and anxieties often surface more strongly during times of stress or change. Candle Face's appearances coincided with those periods in my life, which suggests a link between my emotional state and the intensity of her presence.

Looking back, it seems clear that Candle Face was a complex psychological response to the challenges and fears I faced as a child. She was a construct of my mind, a way to cope with and make sense of the world around me. As I've grown and processed these experiences, Candle Face has receded, at least until recently, which suggests that the need for this imaginary figure has lessened as my understanding and coping mechanisms have changed.

Candle Face was a very real and terrifying presence in my childhood. The evidence, as I see it now, points to her as a manifestation of my inner world. That's what the human mind can do when it's pushed hard enough. As I've come to terms with my past, I've also come to see Candle Face as part of me, a creation of my imagination a child built to survive what he couldn't yet understand.

DISTINGUISHING REALITY FROM IMAGINATION: THE CANDLE FACE DEBATE (PART 2)

July 8, 2024

SPOILER ALERT: This journal entry contains information about characters and themes in *The Empty Lot Next Door*. **If you want to avoid spoilers, stop here until you've finished the book. Reading this journal entry may reveal plot details you may prefer to discover on your own.**

This is the second entry in a two-part series on the legend of Candle Face, an evil entity that haunted my childhood. In the first journal entry, I examined the possibility that Candle Face was a manifestation of past trauma rooted in my own mind. In this second journal entry, I examine the possibility that Candle Face is a genuine ghostly presence, separate from human psychology.

As you read these two accounts, weigh the evidence and decide for yourself whether Candle Face is a supernatural entity or a manifestation of my past trauma.

In my memoir *The Empty Lot Next Door*, I write as Ray, my childhood name, and recount my experiences with Candle Face. I still find myself grappling with the question of her reality. Over the years, I've faced skepticism and disbelief, with many suggesting that Candle Face was a figment of my childhood imagination, a byproduct of fear, stress, or loneliness. Every time I reflect on those encounters, I grow more convinced that Candle Face was an actual entity whose existence and interactions with me and those around me can't be dismissed as imaginary.

Let's consider the consistency and detail in my encounters with Candle Face. A child's imagination can run wild, yet the detail and consistency of Candle Face's appearances, actions, and effects went far beyond what I would expect from a young mind. From Candle Face's evil presence in the empty lot next to my house to the way she entered my home, there was a startling vividness to her appearance. She had a form, a method, and a clear pattern in her actions.

My experiences with Candle Face didn't occur in isolation. They continued over a long period. If she were merely a product of my imagination, it would be difficult to maintain such a consistent and evolving story over time. The way she interacted with the environment, leaving physical marks, and the way she was perceived under different circumstances added to the sense that she was real. For example, her ability to leave cuts on my skin or manipulate physical objects in my bedroom is hard to attribute to imagination alone.

Another reason I believe Candle Face was real is the fact that others, particularly my brother Ricky, shared those experiences. If Candle Face were merely a figment of my imagination, it would be hard to explain Ricky also interacting with her. His reactions and the fear he showed were genuine and independent of my own experiences. This shared perception supports the argument that Candle Face existed outside my own mind.

The emotional and psychological impact of these encounters was profound and lasting, extending well into my adulthood. The fear and anxiety Candle Face caused lasted long after the encounters on my mental health and my sense of safety. The depth of that impact points, at least to me, toward an encounter with something real.

The specific knowledge that Candle Face seemed to possess also supports her reality. She knew personal details and future events that I couldn't have known or predicted, suggesting a level of awareness beyond a mental construct. Her statements about future events and knowledge about personal aspects of my life were later confirmed. That is difficult for me to explain as the product of my subconscious.

The physical evidence, such as the injuries I sustained and the disturbances in the environment around me, is also hard to explain away as imaginary. The scratches on my skin, the disruption in my room, and the changes in the physical space around me during her visits suggest an external force.

Candle Face's presence and actions also seemed to follow a purpose or intent. Imaginary figures are often more chaotic or nonsensical. Her actions seemed deliberate, often with a clear goal, whether to scare, warn, or communicate something specific. That sense of purpose made her feel like an actual entity.

The nature of her appearances and the conditions under which they occurred also suggest she was real. Candle Face often appeared under specific circumstances and in particular locations, following patterns that felt consistent and recognizable. Her appearances were often tied to specific emotional states or events. That pattern suggests a response to something real and identifiable.

I understand why some might view Candle Face as a product of my overactive imagination. The evidence and experiences I've recounted lead me to a different conclusion. The consistency, detail, shared experiences, physical evidence, and lasting impact all point to Candle Face as an actual supernatural entity. Her presence in my life was a tangible, if mysterious, force that left a permanent mark on my childhood and changed how I see the world.

CANDLE FACE CHRONICLES PODCAST: DISTINGUISHING REALITY FROM IMAGINATION - THE CANDLE FACE DEBATE

July 11, 2024

https://youtu.be/D7IYlWdRsvA

Is Candle Face a manifestation of my childhood trauma or a real supernatural entity? In this video, I share my personal experiences and ask you to decide for yourself.

CANDLE FACE VICTIM #36: THE ASSASSIN'S CONFESSION

July 12, 2024

Tired from all the Hurricane Beryl cleanup, I decided to turn in early. The hours I usually waste on Facebook and YouTube could wait until tomorrow night. I turned off the living room light but left the kitchen light on, keeping a patch of shadow in the far corner for any Lost Soul that might want to visit. Just as I laid my head on the pillow, the shadow pulsed. I wasn't in the mood for this. Not tonight. But I had a job to do. With a sigh, I sat up and got ready. An old man in his late sixties wearing a cowboy hat stepped out of the shadow and came toward me. Then he began.

I'm your standard grumpy old man. I hate everybody. I hate nearly everything. My "wife," and I use that word lightly, nags all damn day. She tells me I never gave her the life she wanted and that every bad thing in her life is my fault. When I get tired of hearing it, I pull this big cowboy hat down low so folks won't look me in the face, then I get in my van and drive. I used to wish I could disappear. Funny thing is, I did. Just not the way I had in mind.

One day, after I'd heard all I could stand, I got in my van and headed to a gas station. I was fixin' to get on I-35 and leave the nagging behind for a while. I pumped my gas, went inside for coffee and snacks, and came back out to black helicopters easing over my van. I could see men inside in military-type uniforms, dropping ropes down over the roof.

I knew what it was. I knew they were coming for me. I'm no stranger to the law. I've been in and out of jail for years for the things I got caught doing.

He stopped and sat there smiling to himself like he'd wandered into a pleasant memory. I cleared my throat to get him moving again.

"I figured my run was over," he said. "Figured I'd spend the rest of my life in prison."

"Why? What did you do? Why would they want you?" I asked.

His eyes widened. Then he glanced back toward the shadow he had come through.

The shadow in the corner grew, and the kitchen light started to flicker.

"Quick, turn on the living room light," he said.

I hesitated.

"Now."

I jumped up and turned it on.

The room lit up, though the bulbs still flickered. I sat back down. So did he. I knew what we had just done would cost me later, but I didn't care. I had a job to do.

"I used to kill for Candle Face," he said. "Back in the seventies and eighties. We didn't call her that back then."

"Why did you stop killing for her?" I asked.

"I lost my taste for it. When I first started, she was good to me. She made me feel like I was somebody. I'd do her work, and she'd answer. Then that dried up. I kept killing, thinking the next one would get her attention. It didn't. I was turning into just another killer. Years later, my wife told me Candle Face would come for me one day. I told her I didn't care. So I quit. The last one I did was in the summer of 1987."

"Who did you kill?"

"I don't remember her name. Asian woman. Those Asian names are hard to remember."

"Tell me about her. What happened?"

"A fellow Deliverer asked me to ride with him on one near Killeen. I'd already finished my own list, so I went along anyway. He was good. Not just at killing. At working over the Marked before he took them in. We got in a car he'd stolen and headed that way."

"You said Deliverer and the Marked," I said. "What are they?"

He looked at me, then at the dim shadow.

"Deliverers are the ones who've proven themselves. We hunt the unbelievers, the Marked, and take them to Mother's Lair."

"I've heard that name before," I said. "Mother."

"Yeah," he said. "Her children call her that. But don't get this twisted. Her children are all those in her Lair. But she doesn't treat all her children the same. She favors the Tlazopilli and hates the Icnopilli."

"Anyway," he went on, "we got lucky. Saw her out walking in her neighborhood. We jumped out, dragged her into the car, drove her past Copperas Cove, killed her, buried her, and laid big rocks over the grave. Nobody ever found her."

He stopped again with that same satisfied look on his face. Then we both heard soft footsteps upstairs while the lights flickered again.

"It's just my son upstairs," I said.

"Anyway, we drove back to Austin. It was a satisfying kill, but I was done. I don't kill for free. I killed for Candle Face's attention, and she wasn't giving it anymore. So that Asian woman was my last."

"How were you killed?" I asked. I reached over and touched his right arm to see whether he still had flesh. He did.

"I got sick of my wife's nagging one day and got in my van. I stopped for gas."

"Oh, is this when you saw the black helicopters?"

"Yeah. That's it. When I saw them, I called my wife and told her my past had finally caught up with me. The helicopters dropped lower. Their rotors pounded so hard I could barely hear her on the phone. Then the side doors opened and men in tactical gear came down the ropes fast. They hit the pavement running and boxed me in. One of them threw a rope around my neck, and before I knew it, I was off my feet. I was choking while they hauled me up."

"They hanged you? That doesn't sound like police work," I said.

"That's how I remember it. I know now that Candle Face did it."

"So how did you really die? The police didn't do that."

"I don't know. I only know what I saw and felt. That rope felt real enough. I was hoping you could figure out the rest for me."

"Why should I help you? You were a mass murderer."

He looked down at his hands.

"Maybe you shouldn't. Maybe I deserve what I've got waiting on me. But I can still help you help the other Lost Souls."

"How?"

"Ray, I just did," he said with a grin and a soft laugh. "Now turn off the light and let me go back. It's where I belong, I guess."

I stood up and switched off the living room light.

The old man walked toward the shadow as it swelled again in the far corner. Just before he reached it, he turned back and spoke quickly.

"Ray, the arms that are about to drag me in belong to the man who was with me when we killed that Asian woman."

The pull was savage. The arms jerked him back in hard enough to snap his body sideways and slam him against the edge of the portal before swallowing him whole. His boots kicked wildly for a second, scraping at the floor, then vanished into the black. One strangled scream burst out of him just before the shadow sealed shut.

The living room went silent except for my own heavy breathing. The shadow in the corner seemed to shrink back to its normal size as if it had satisfied its hunger for now. I stood there for a moment, staring at where the old man had disappeared.

Personal Note to My Readers

This testimony gave me several new terms, and I don't think any of them were used loosely. The old man used Deliverer as if it were a rank. From the way he spoke, Deliverers go after the Marked, the living who reject Candle Face and draw her attention. They take them to the Lair.

He also used the name Mother. I have heard that word before from other Lost Souls, but this time it came with more shape. Candle Face is spoken of as the head of a family. That family is divided. Some serve her. Some are taken by her.

That brought me back to Icnopilli. Earlier, Candle Face used that word for one of the Lost Souls. After tracing the sound and narrowing the spelling, I found a Nahuatl word that fits. If I heard her correctly, the Lost Souls may be the Icnopilli, the abandoned children, the children kept in the Lair. After that, I went back to the same line of research looking for a term that might fit the children she favors. Tlazopilli may be that word. If I'm reading this correctly, the Tlazopilli would be the children she recognizes as her own, the ones she raises above the others. Deliverers may fall into that side of the hierarchy.

I'm still putting this together, but the outline is getting clearer. Mother stands at the top. The Tlazopilli appear to be her favored children. The Deliverers work under her and go after the Marked. The Icnopilli may be the Lost Souls, the children taken into the Lair and held there. I can't say yet whether these words came from Candle Face herself or whether her followers built this language around her later. What I can say is that each new testimony is giving me more of her internal order, and that order is starting to explain how she separates the children she uses from the children she keeps.

CANDLE FACE CHRONICLES PODCAST: MR. SMOE'S STORY

July 24, 2024

https://youtu.be/SfEcgv7sefk

Watch our interview with "Mr. Smoe," a self-proclaimed Candle Face Disciple who says she saved him from suicide decades ago. Join us as we piece together his story and examine what it may tell us about Candle Face.

CANDLE FACE CHRONICLES PODCAST: THE UNTOLD STORY OF CANDLE FACE VICTIM #3

July 31, 2024

https://youtu.be/J1AZpj_qMaE

This episode covers Candle Face Victim #3: Sixth Street to the Gravel Pit. A devoted podcast listener may have identified the victims. We continue the investigation in the hope of finding justice and closure.

THE END OF CANDLE FACE CHRONICLES PODCAST AND A NEW DIRECTION

August 9, 2024

I need to announce the end of the Candle Face Chronicles podcast after only six episodes. This decision hasn't been easy, and it's one I've struggled with, but I believe it's necessary.

Candle Face Chronicles has been a deeply personal mission for me to bring peace to the Lost Souls Candle Face has killed or ordered her followers to kill. This mission has consumed my thoughts, driven my actions, often at the cost of my peace of mind, and drained me financially. The seriousness of this project demands a platform and an audience that take the paranormal seriously.

Through the Get Haunted Network, I had the privilege of connecting with a community of people, Rob, Sara, Courtney, Trevor, Stacey Tallitsch, Ernie and Denise Pack, Wade Kirby, Richard Breault, and many others who shared their passion and support along the way. The Get Haunted Network is a strong community with shows that explore the paranormal with curiosity and humor. It's a place for those who enjoy paranormal entertainment, and I highly recommend it. My work with *Candle Face Chronicles* has led me in a different direction, one that requires a more serious focus on the Lost Souls' stories and the nature of the paranormal. The lighthearted tone of the Get Haunted Network doesn't seem like the right place for an entity that haunts and kills her prey.

Recently, I had an experience that made me rethink my approach. The friends and family of a victim featured on my podcast reached out and asked that I stop discussing their loved one. The pain in their voices was unmistakable. Listening to them ask for understanding was overwhelming. I was overcome with guilt as I realized the pain my words had unintentionally caused. I knew my search for truth had reopened wounds that had barely begun to heal.

I couldn't sleep that night. All I could hear were the voices of the living, those who are still here and still hurting. Their grief and their pleas for compassion made it clear that my approach must change. The voices of the living have to come first.

This experience has confirmed a fear I've had since the beginning: that the sensitive nature of *Candle Face Chronicles* may be too much for those who knew and loved the victims. I've mentioned this concern in several of my podcast episodes, but it took this call for me to fully understand its impact. As a result, I'll no longer provide the names of those I believe to be victims of Candle Face. My focus will now shift toward locating their remains without publicly identifying them, in an effort to spare their loved ones more pain.

I'm also deeply concerned about the possibility of wrongly implicating innocent people as killers. The Lost Souls have been providing more detailed testimonies lately, including information about Candle Face's followers who have killed for her. There's always the risk that these details could be inaccurate and lead to innocent people being identified as killers. Because of that, I won't publicly identify those the Lost Souls claim are responsible for their deaths. My focus will remain on helping the Lost Souls find peace without causing further harm to the living.

As I move forward, I plan to focus more on understanding Candle Face herself, investigating her origins and methods in greater depth. To do this, I'll work closely with paranormal investigators, psychics, and mediums in the Austin area, where much of Candle Face's activity has centered. I also intend to explore historical records, folklore, and ancient texts for clues that may reveal Candle Face's origins. Understanding where she comes from may give us the key to stopping her.

The broader community still matters in this effort. While I plan to distance myself from the online paranormal community, which often focuses on entertainment, I'll continue to crowdsource ideas from those who have been following *Candle Face Chronicles* closely. Your theories, tips, and observations may offer useful leads, and together we may discover new ways to weaken or even banish Candle Face.

I'll also speak with religious leaders in hopes of gaining a fuller understanding of how to help the Lost Souls and stop Candle Face. This mission has to be about finding real solutions for those suffering from Candle Face.

At this point, I'm filled with regret and hope. I regret any pain I have caused, and I hope these Lost Souls can finally find peace. The podcast has come to an end. My work hasn't. The search for answers and the mission to bring peace to the Lost Souls continue. I may periodically do live videos from the locations where the Lost Souls have guided me and conduct interviews, but these will focus on the work itself and avoid identifying the victims or killers. This approach will let me continue respectfully and compassionately without causing further distress to the families of the Lost Souls or implicating possibly innocent people in their deaths.

To the Get Haunted Network and everyone who has supported me, thank you. Your encouragement and belief in this mission have meant a lot to me. I hope you'll continue with me as I look for better ways to do this work, with compassion and respect guiding it.

SHIFTING FOCUS TO SUPERNATURAL READERS

September 03, 2024

My last journal entry was on August 9, 2024, when I decided to stop the Candle Face Chronicles podcast. This decision wasn't easy, and I felt it was necessary. I truly enjoyed my time with the Get Haunted Network. Over time, I began to realize it wasn't serious enough for a topic this grave. *Candle Face Chronicles* requires a focus that treats this mission with the seriousness it deserves: finding the Lost Souls' remains and identifying their killers.

Then a family member of one of the Lost Souls called me, and that changed the feel of everything. She begged me to stop discussing her loved one because she couldn't bear the pain of knowing Candle Face was torturing them. The guilt was overwhelming, and I began to wonder if Candle Face was haunting me and driving me crazy the same way she haunts her victims. Many of her victims commit suicide or go mad because she gets into their heads. Is this her way of getting into mine?

A few nights ago, after nearly a month of silence, a Lost Soul visited me and told me I must continue my mission of helping the Lost Souls and not give up, because they're relying on me. That visit helped me realize that I must press on. How do I continue searching for their bodies and identifying their killers without publicly naming the Lost Souls and their killers?

I've devised a new strategy to move forward without causing more pain to their living relatives and friends.

I believe the key lies in partnering with supernatural readers, who bring curiosity, persistence, and a willingness to confront Candle Face. I've tried collaborating with paranormal investigators, psychics, and mediums in the past, and those efforts haven't given me the results I hoped for. Many in the paranormal community prefer to focus on cases that are less complex or intense than Candle Face. They tend to stay within their comfort zones. Their contributions are still important, but Candle Face requires an investigation that goes further than typical paranormal encounters.

Supernatural readers engage with their books and continue reading even when frightened. They may pull the covers up closer or snuggle with their partner while continuing to read. The paranormal community tends to run at the first unknown knock or thump. These readers have a unique advantage: they're used to solving puzzles and following complex threads in the paranormal world through stories. Their persistence comes from curiosity and commitment to the story. By bringing them into the investigation, I can use their perceptions to help work through the clues left by the Lost Souls. I'll use a private Facebook group and a public Facebook page for these serious supernatural readers:

- The private Facebook group will be for those who want to engage with more sensitive and confidential aspects of the investigation. Here, I can share specific details about the Lost Souls, working directly with families who have given consent, without publicly revealing their identities. Readers will have access to more detailed information, and their contributions will directly affect the progress of the investigation.

- The public Facebook page will allow for more general collaboration. I'll share clues, such as locations, objects, and cryptic messages, allowing readers to help solve cases without revealing specific names or details unless authorized by the Lost Souls' relatives. This will protect living relatives and friends from further grief and still involve the public in a meaningful way.

To balance the need for closure with the need to protect families, I'll use several tactics:

1. **Permission from Families:** Before publicly naming any lost soul, I'll seek permission from the family. If they're uncomfortable with public disclosure, I'll keep the investigation focused on anonymous details and still work privately to bring resolution.

2. **Pseudonyms for Public Cases:** If permission isn't granted, I'll use pseudonyms or vague descriptions to refer to the Lost

Souls (e.g., "A woman from Austin, Texas, who went missing in 2010"). This allows readers to stay engaged with the investigation and protects the identity of the victims.

3. **Private Updates for Families:** Families will still be kept informed of progress and milestones privately, even if the public doesn't get all the details. They'll receive the closure they need without the emotional burden of a public case.

4. **Separate Public and Private Information:** Public posts will focus on general clues and updates. More specific, confidential information will be shared as needed for those engaging in the private group. This way, the investigation continues without crossing sensitive lines.

5. **Milestone Updates for Readers:** Readers won't need to know the personal identities of the Lost Souls to contribute. They'll still receive updates on important milestones, such as locating remains or solving a critical piece of the puzzle, so they know they played a role in helping the Lost Souls find peace.

6. **Work with Trusted Mediators:** In some cases, I'll rely on mediators between the families and me, ensuring that sensitive information is handled with care and that families are comfortable with what's shared publicly.

7. **Delayed Disclosure:** For particularly sensitive cases, I may wait until a case is fully resolved before releasing any information to the public. This allows the family time to process the findings before anything is made public and may help prevent emotional distress.

These steps should help protect families and still allow the investigation to continue with the help of supernatural readers.

Besides collaborating with supernatural readers, I'll seek the help of spiritual leaders from various faiths. By bringing in voices from different religious traditions, I can better understand the spiritual dimensions of Candle Face and the Lost Souls. Spiritual leaders can offer guidance on rituals, prayers, and spiritual protections that might help in the investigation. Their involvement can also help guide how to proceed with respect for different spiritual beliefs. Involving these leaders may give the investigation a wider range of spiritual tools and practices that could help combat Candle Face and bring peace to the Lost Souls.

I'll also consider seeking help from historians and folklorists who can provide context to Candle Face's origins. Understanding the historical and cultural background of the areas where Candle Face operates might reveal important clues about her identity and methods. Additionally, working with experts in psychology, particularly those who specialize in trauma and the paranormal, could help decode the experiences of the Lost Souls and offer new ways to support them.

By involving these collaborators, including spiritual leaders, historians, folklorists, and psychologists, the investigation can take a broader approach that addresses the physical, emotional, and spiritual aspects of Candle Face's terror.

I'll still seek help from paranormal investigators, psychics, and mediums, especially from the Central Texas paranormal community, as Candle Face's attacks seem to be concentrated there. Their input will remain valuable. My primary focus will be on readers and collaborators who bring persistence, curiosity, and a strong commitment to helping the Lost Souls and understanding the origins of Candle Face. That is the direction I believe gives this investigation the best chance of moving forward without causing more harm to the living.

CANDLE FACE VICTIM #37: DJ OF THE DAMNED

September 13, 2024

I picked up my extra-long white blanket, fluffing it high into the air so it could spread out fully, almost floating like a ghost before it drifted down toward the couch, my bed for over a year and a half now. I can't even remember what a real bed feels like, and frankly, I don't care. This couch is perfect for me.

But as the blanket began to settle, something felt wrong. It didn't land flat like it always did. At that moment, the lights in the room flickered violently, casting strange, shifting shadows across the walls. My heart skipped a beat, and the blanket, now halfway to the couch, revealed a faint outline, disturbingly human-like, pressing up against the fabric, as though the couch itself had suddenly taken on a body.

My pulse quickened as I stared at the form taking shape beneath the blanket, waiting for it to move. But it stayed perfectly still.

Fear crept over me for the first time in a long while, even though I knew it was just another nocturnal visitor, the first in two months, the longest drought. Slowly, I pulled the blanket back. There was nothing there, just the distinct impression of something that had been lying there moments ago. I took a few steps back, my pulse thumping in my chest, and watched as the imprint shifted, flattening and then rising slightly, as if someone had sat up. I could clearly make out the shape of what looked like a seated figure, the faint depression of where its body had been.

Then I heard a voice, crackling like static through an old radio.

"Hello, Ray. I need your help."

"Where are you?" I asked, my voice trembling as the temperature in the room rose.

"I don't have a physical form anymore, just a voice. People all around Austin knew my voice in the '90s, but few knew what I looked like. Candle Face took my body because..." The voice paused. "She took my body because I used it to hide my filth, my dirty deeds. She took it away to strip me bare, to punish me for the lies I told. She left my voice because that's all I ever was, a voice with no substance. And now she's made sure I can never have a body again."

He then started his testimony.

> I worked as a DJ in Austin in the '90s. Everyone knew my voice, but no one knew my struggles. I was addicted to porn and enjoyed flashing people around 6th Street. I'd find drunk girls wandering back to their cars through the nearby alleys and open my trench coat. Then I'd run

away. None of my listeners knew about my dirty secret, making it even more exciting.

He paused momentarily.

I loved the adrenaline rush leading up to the moment I exposed myself and watched the girls' reactions. The idea that they probably listened to me on the radio but had no idea it was me made me want to explode. I lived for that thrill. But eventually, I got caught. Somehow, I managed to hide the truth from everyone, my bosses, my listeners, and even my friends and family.

He stopped for a moment, as though struggling to continue.

After a year, I started to feel the urge again. I tried to resist it, but it took a lot of meth to stop me from acting out. One day, a woman handed me a flyer on 6th Street about a little girl. The flyer said she could free people from their pain if they only believed. I kept the flyer, folding it neatly to fit in my wallet. I read it over and over, as if it held some answer to my misery.

One day, the same woman who handed out the flyers recognized me. She asked if I had given it any thought. I showed her the flyer, and she seemed so impressed that I kept it with me. She even shed a tear or two. We started talking, some light flirting, and I thought maybe I'd get lucky. But it didn't happen that night. We met up several more times over the following weeks. She wanted to know all about me and what being a radio star was like.

One day, she brought up the little girl again. She said I could help spread her message with a weekly radio show. I had no interest in doing a show about a little girl ghost who supposedly heals people's pain, but I played along. I only wanted to get with her. We kept meeting, and she kept pushing for the show. I told her it would start soon, knowing I was lying just to keep her attention. Eventually, I told her the first episode would air that night, but the truth was, I wasn't working on it at all.

His voice trembled slightly, as if recalling a memory he desperately wanted to forget.

When I arrived at her apartment, it seemed normal at first. She smiled, pulled me in for a kiss, and I thought I had won. But then she pulled the curtains back. Outside, I saw figures standing just beyond the windows in the dark. The same people who handed out the flyers. They were watching us. Silent. Waiting.

My kitchen lights flickered again as he continued.

She told me she knew I was lying about the show. They knew. They knew I was only interested in her, that I was stringing them along. They dragged me down, and she pulled out a knife. The others held me down while she cut into me, carving symbols into my skin. They said I would now serve her. She would take away my physical form and leave me as nothing more than a voice.

The static in his voice grew louder, more desperate.

She left my radio-like voice because that's all I ever had. All I ever was, a voice with no substance. Now, I serve that little girl in her Lair. I'm the voice in many of her victims' ears.

There's a woman right now in Austin who ridiculed her. She believes her baby died peacefully of natural causes. But every night, I yell a different story into her ears. I tell her the truth: that the one you call "Candle Face" took her child. I tell her how, in the dead of night, the baby was snatched from her crib, its tiny body twisted and broken in ways no mother should ever imagine. I describe the sound of its last breath.

Every night, I make her hear the baby's cries. The sound had none of a newborn's soft cooing. It came out as tortured wails of someone caught in a meat grinder. I tell her the cries are coming from the other side, louder every night, louder the longer she stays awake. She thinks if she keeps her eyes open, the cries will stop, but they never do. I make sure of that.

Sometimes, she'll claw at her ears until they bleed, desperate to drown out the sound of her baby's torture. She's afraid to sleep because when she does, I make the cries even more vivid.

When I let her sleep, she dreams. She sees her baby reaching for her, its tiny fingers blackened and stiff, its eyes empty. She tries to hold it, but the baby crumbles in her arms, a pile of ash. And still, she hears the screams, louder and louder, until she wakes up, sobbing and gasping for air, wishing for death.

The truth is, Ray, she's already gone. She doesn't know it, but she's lost her mind. I've hollowed her out. I've turned her into a shell, and soon, she'll do anything to silence the cries, even if it means joining her baby.

The kitchen lights flickered again.

And there's a man, a doctor. People trusted him with their lives. But he mocked the little girl. Now, I make him hear the voices of every patient he's ever lost on the operating table, their voices twisted with pain and betrayal, as if they knew he could have saved them but didn't.

Every night, I shout their last words into his ears. The desperate gasps, the pleas for him to keep trying, even when their hearts had already stopped. He can hear the machines flatlining, the beeps echoing in his head. I remind him of every mistake, every hesitation that led to their deaths. I make him relive every incision, every cut that went too deep, every moment where he hesitated, those seconds that cost them their lives.

One patient was a young girl, no older than six. She went into surgery for something routine, a procedure he'd done hundreds of times. But when she didn't wake up, her parents never forgave him. Now, every night, I make him hear her voice, soft at first. "Doctor..." she says, "I can't breathe... why didn't you save me?" He tries to answer her, but his throat closes up. She keeps saying, "You let me die... why didn't you save me?"

Another voice belongs to a man who had a heart attack on the table. His surgery was supposed to be his last chance, but the doctor's hands slipped during the operation, severing an artery. The man bled out in minutes. Now, I make him feel the blood on his hands, warm and sticky, as the patient's voice comes through, gurgling, choking. "Why did you let me die?" the voice asks, over and over, in a wet rasp. "I wasn't ready."

It's always the same, Ray. The voices start soft. But by midnight, they're screaming. They scream his name, they beg for him to help them again, they accuse him of playing God. Sometimes, I make him feel their hands, cold and clammy, grabbing at his shoulders, pulling at his wrists, dragging him back to the operating table. He feels their fingers digging into his skin, trying to drag him down with them.

He doesn't sleep anymore. He can't. Every time he closes his eyes, I make him see their faces, gray, lifeless, staring at him from the cold steel of the operating table. Their mouths gape open, and screams pour out. Sometimes, I show him their corpses, rising from the table, the gaping wounds he gave them still raw, bleeding, as they reach out to him, yelling, "You should have saved me."

He thought he could hide, tried to drown himself in alcohol, pills, anything to quiet the voices, but they follow him. I follow him. She follows him. He's already seeing shadows, thinking he's catching glimpses of them standing at the foot of his bed. But he knows. No matter where he goes, I'll find him. They'll find him. They're always waiting for him to slip up, waiting for the moment when he'll be the one lying on the table, with no one to save him.

That's the beauty of it, Ray. He can't save himself. No one can.

His voice grew more intense.

I'm the voice that reminds them, Ray. I'm the voice that keeps her, Candle Face, alive in their heads. I tailor each story, spinning it just right to dig deep into their worst fears, their darkest regrets. I get into their heads, using my DJ voice, planting seeds of terror until they break.

I tried to speak, but my voice was barely audible. "Why... why are you telling me this?"

"Because, Ray," his voice crackled, "it'll be your turn soon enough. You're already hearing me, aren't you? Candle Face sees you, and trust me, she's in your head. You just don't realize it yet."

My throat tightened, and I tried to breathe.

"Soon I'll be yelling into your ears," the DJ continued, his voice shifting from desperate to almost gleeful. "Maybe I'll tell you that the people you trust are turning against you. Maybe I'll make you see Candle Face's victims in every face you pass. Or maybe I'll make you doubt everything, your memories, your thoughts, until you can't tell what's real anymore. That's when the fun begins, Ray."

"And you know, when I'm done with you, Ray, I'll be promoted. She rewards those who serve her well. I'll become one of her shadows, the ones who torment her critics when they arrive at her Lair. But first, I get to toy with you. I'll make you feel like you're burning alive, your skin peeling off as you scream. And then I'll take away everything you hold dear, one piece at a time. Your sanity? Gone. Your life? I'll make you beg for the end, but it'll never come."

He paused.

"Do you know what else will happen, Ray? Your stories, the characters you created in your books, they'll haunt you. Every twisted plotline, every agony you wrote into their lives, they'll inflict on you tenfold. All Candle Face's victims will also come to you. They'll all start to blame you for their agony. The woman who lost her child will come to you every night, cradling her broken baby and asking you why you did it. No matter how much you plead that it was just fiction, she won't care. She'll leave that lifeless child in your arms, and you'll hear the cries you made her hear too, louder and louder, until your mind shatters under the weight of her pain."

"Remember the doctor, Ray? He'll come for you too. You'll be the one lying on the operating table, feeling his botched surgeries, over and over again, each cut leaving you closer to death but never letting you die. You'll scream for mercy, but just like in your story, there will be none."

His laughter echoed in the living room.

"And Candle Face, as you call her, oh, she'll enjoy this most of all. You think you've been writing about her, don't you? But she's been writing about you, Ray. She's already in your head, twisting every thought, and soon, you won't be able to tell what's real and what's fiction. You'll see her in every corner of your mind, hear her voice in every silence, feel her hot breath in every nightmare. And the worst part? You'll never escape."

My heart pounded in my chest, and for the first time, I realized that the stories I'd written, the horrors I'd conjured, were coming back for me.

Tears welled up in my eyes.

"When I'm done with you, Ray, you'll wish you had never jumped in that hole. You'll wish you had never given her that nasty name. But by then, it'll be too late. You'll be too far gone."

I stood there, trembling, as his voice faded into silence. For the first time in a long time, I felt the walls of my mind closing in, and the thought that crept into my mind terrified me more than any spirit ever had: I need to focus on my own sanity before I become one of the Lost Souls myself.

Personal Note to My Readers

To all of you following my mission, I feel it's time to share the truth that I've been grappling with, truths I wish I could bury, but they won't stay hidden. Candle Face has been in my life far longer than I ever imagined. This mission to help the Lost Souls trapped in her Lair has become something I can barely comprehend. I've written their stories, shared their pain, and tried to give them the peace they deserve, but now I fear that trying to save them has brought me closer to becoming one of them.

Each night, the voices grow louder, and the shadows feel closer. I can't escape the feeling that it's no longer just about helping the souls who cry out to me. It's about saving myself. I need to protect myself as much as I've tried to protect them. Candle Face is no longer content with taking her critics. She's coming for me, using the DJ, using her victims, and soon enough, she'll break into my mind fully.

It's a cruel irony, isn't it? I still believe that helping these Lost Souls is the key. I've convinced myself that if I pick up the pace, if I help more of them, maybe it'll stop. Maybe I'll have done enough to quiet the voices, to end this nightmare before it consumes me. But then again, I don't even know what to believe anymore. My mind plays tricks on me, twisting reality into something unrecognizable.

I'm haunted by the very souls I've tried to save. I hear their cries now, which is something I haven't written before. They accuse me, blame me, ask why I didn't do more. And Candle Face, she's in my head now. She's writing about me as much as I've written about her. What will she do with her story about me? What does it say?

I don't know how much longer I can stand on this tightrope, balancing between protecting the Lost Souls and protecting myself. Maybe there's no protection at all. Maybe it's all part of Candle Face's game, and I'm just next. I have mentioned this before, but this time, I know I can't escape.

To my readers, I want to say thank you for standing by me. But I fear that soon, I won't be able to stand at all. The shadows are closing in, and I'm not sure if I can hold on. I need to focus on my own sanity before I become one of the Lost Souls myself. But even as I write these words, I know my time is running out. Candle Face is already here, and the battle for my mind is well underway.

Stay safe, and pray for the Lost Souls. Pray for me.

CANDLE FACE VICTIM #38: HIGH ON DRUGS, LOW ON BELIEF

September 20, 2024

Things have been hectic lately. Yesterday, Mr. Smoe called me a liar. He wants to appear on a podcast with me again to expose what he claims are lies and reveal Candle Face's "real" identity. It's hard not to let his words get under my skin. After everything I've been through, after all the Lost Souls who have come to me, he thinks this is all some elaborate lie?

What exactly does Mr. Smoe think he knows? What is he planning to say on the podcast? Worse, what if people believe him? He's convinced he has the truth about Candle Face, claiming he'll reveal her "real" identity. I've decided it's better to let him say his piece without my interference. I won't challenge his claims right now. For now, I'll hold back what I know.

Hopefully, we can do this podcast soon. These accusations will only fester the longer they hang in the air. And I can't afford to let them distract me from my mission, not when so much is at stake.

Sitting on my couch and makeshift bed, I thought about what Mr. Smoe said. As the hours dragged on, the lights began to flicker, and the shadows in the corner of my living room thickened. Signs that a lost soul had arrived. Out of the shadows stepped a woman in her mid-thirties, wearing a wide smile framed by dark red lipstick. She sat beside me on the couch, bouncing a little as if trying to get comfortable. Her eyes scanned me, still smiling.

> "I'm a fellow veteran," she said. "So, I hope you'll give me special attention and help me find my killers."

> "How can I help you?" I asked, without thinking.

> Her smile faltered, her voice softening. "I guess I should start with my name. It's Katty."

> At least, I thought she said "Katty," but something about the way she mumbled it, or maybe it was just the flickering lights distracting me, made me unsure. Later, I could've sworn I heard her refer to herself as Matty. Was it Katty or Matty? I couldn't tell.

> She continued, oblivious to my confusion. "I had a good life once. You know, I was happy. I served my country. It all went downhill when I started hanging with some Soldiers in my unit at Fort Hood."

"They were using drugs," she went on, "and I wasn't planning to get back into that scene after fighting so hard to stay clean. But you know how it goes. Old habits die hard." She paused, her eyes dropping as she seemed to relive the struggle. "They had these civilian friends off base, and that's where I started getting cheaper stuff. We'd all hang out there, staying up all night, high as a kite, talking about everything. Politics, life, the future. When you're high, you think you're solving all the world's problems. It was all so stupid. But when you're in that state, you believe you're invincible. Like nothing can touch you."

Her eyes shifted up to meet mine again. "That's when Candle Face came up."

I leaned in slightly, curious about where this was going. She caught my movement and continued.

"They were always talking about her, this spirit who would come for people who doubted her. I didn't believe it, though. I mean, how could I? I thought it was just some dumb story to scare each other, you know? But I played along. You kinda have to when you're in with a group like that. You don't want to be the odd one out."

She stopped for a moment.

"And I needed them," she said softly. "I needed the drugs."

"What happened next?" I asked.

"I screwed up," she said. "One night, we were sitting around, high as usual, talking about Candle Face like always. This time, I wasn't really paying attention, and I let it slip. I said, 'I don't really believe in this Candle Face stuff. It's all stupid, isn't it?'" She paused, as if reliving that moment. "That's when everything changed. They all went quiet. I'll never forget the look in their eyes. They looked angry, like I had broken some sacred rule. But they didn't say anything right then. They just stared."

She took a deep breath. "I didn't think much of it at first," she said, her voice trembling. "I thought maybe they were just messing with me. But after that night, things started to feel off. They weren't laughing anymore, not around me. And they weren't as friendly. Like they were keeping their distance."

Her eyes filled with fear as she continued. "Every time we got together after that, they wouldn't joke around with me like before. No more late-night conversations, no more small talk. I'd catch them glancing at each other when I'd speak, like I didn't belong anymore. Like I was an outsider."

She swallowed hard. "Then, one night, they invited me to hang out again. But this time, it wasn't at the usual spot. They came to my house near Killeen." Her voice dropped to a whisper. "I should've known something was wrong."

She wiped her palms against her jeans. "When they showed up, the vibe was different. They weren't there to get high or talk about life. They had this look like they were there on a mission."

She hesitated, her voice breaking. "They told me it was Candle Face's will. That she demanded punishment for what I'd said. For lying. For pretending to believe when I didn't."

Her eyes filled with tears. "They held me down," she said as she began to cry. "They said they weren't doing it, that Candle Face was making them, that she was controlling their hands. But I know they believed it. They thought they had to do it. And they killed me, right there, in my own home."

She shook her head slowly, tears falling down her cheeks. "Because I didn't believe."

The room fell into silence. I could feel her pain, the betrayal, and the fear that had consumed her in those final moments. Then, as if she couldn't hold it in any longer, she said, "I don't know if Candle Face is real. They believed she was, and that's all that mattered."

I nodded slowly. "I'll help you." I didn't know how, but I would find a way. I owed her that much. Deep down, I knew this would be far from simple. I haven't helped many Lost Souls in the nearly yearlong stretch I've been forced into this role. But I must try.

She stood up and walked to the portal, turning to give me another glance. "Bye Ray, please help me and as many of us as possible." She stood at attention and gave me a sharp salute.

My chest tightened as I stood up and returned the salute. She stepped back into the portal and disappeared.

RACING AGAINST TIME: PREPARING FOR CANDLE FACE'S RETURN

September 21, 2024

Today should be a productive day. I'm heading to San Antonio for the 7th Annual Paranormal Fest 2024 at Victoria's Black Swan Inn. I'm hoping to meet serious paranormal investigators, psychics, and mediums who may be willing to help me with the Lost Souls. I'll also look for people with remote viewing experience who could help with the investigation. Until now, my contact with the paranormal community has been exclusively online. Today, I'll have the chance to meet part of the Texas paranormal community in person.

I've been practicing the remote viewing techniques I learned in Stacey Tallitsch's class, but I think it helps to learn from more than one person. Each teacher uses different methods, and that can broaden my understanding. It's like Investigations 101. Pulling from different sources gives you a clearer picture. Remote viewing also requires discipline and a range of skills, and learning different approaches might help me strengthen the areas where I'm weak.

Next weekend, I'll attend a Mediumship Bootcamp at the Triple Six Social in San Marcos, Texas. Many people from the Get Haunted Network have said I have some medium abilities, but I've never felt confident in them. Hopefully, this bootcamp will help me develop those skills, or at least make me more comfortable with what I may be capable of. Meeting mediums willing to help me with the Lost Souls is also a priority.

In the next few weeks, I plan to branch out and start conversations with religious leaders to broaden my contacts. Understanding their views may help me figure out how to help the Lost Souls and understand Candle Face more clearly. There's a lot I need to do before Candle Face comes for me.

THE CHALLENGE OF SEEKING SUPPORT FOR CANDLE FACE'S VICTIMS

September 22, 2024

Yesterday, September 21, 2024, I attended the 7th Annual Paranormal Fest at the Black Swan Inn in San Antonio. It was my first time at a paranormal festival, and I genuinely enjoyed it. The event was filled with speakers and booths, showcasing a mix of authors, paranormal investigators, psychics, and mediums offering their services.

One of the best parts was meeting a group of paranormal investigators from Paranormal Journal. They seemed genuinely interested in what I had to say about Candle Face. I explained that most paranormal investigators, psychics, and mediums I've met online haven't been interested in Candle Face or helping me with the Lost

Souls. They seemed surprised, given the kind of work I'm trying to do. I mentioned how many groups I've seen on YouTube run at the first sign of something knocking, which prompted one of the Paranormal Journal members to chuckle and say, "We run towards the knocking!" That got a laugh from everyone. I replied, "Everyone says that," which led to even more laughter.

Despite the humor, there was a seriousness in their eyes, something I've only seen from the Houston-based paranormal investigation team, GenX Paranormal Investigations. They stood there listening to me, studying me, and giving me the sense that maybe I'd finally found a San Antonio or Austin area paranormal team willing to help me with the Lost Souls.

Feeling hopeful, I wandered around the venue and spotted a psychic sitting at her booth. I decided to approach her and ask for a reading. She was enthusiastic until I mentioned Candle Face and the Lost Souls. The moment those words left my mouth, her expression shifted, and she quickly told me that she likely couldn't help. I thanked her and moved on, approaching another psychic who, to my surprise, stayed interested even after I mentioned Candle Face. She agreed to do a reading, my first one ever.

The nearly 30-minute session was interesting, but everything she said seemed vague, almost like it could apply to anyone. Tarot readings work that way. They can be interpreted broadly, which is part of what makes them feel personal and accurate. Still, hearing her say things out loud was comforting, like seeing a familiar view from a slightly different angle. Although I didn't get her name, her CashApp information listed her as "Victoria Doane." I'd recommend her to anyone interested in a reading, as she was kind and professional.

She gave me permission to record and post the reading:

https://youtu.be/bVIqrdC1rP4

But I kept thinking that a psychic reading might not give me the specificity I need for the Lost Souls. I'm not dismissing the field. I just think I may need a different approach for the answers I'm seeking.

Interestingly, several psychics, including Victoria, have said that I have latent mediumship abilities that need to be refined. I've heard this before. Maybe I need to stop relying on the paranormal community and develop these abilities myself. The thought of doing it all alone is intimidating, though. My interactive investigation was meant to involve others, to invite people to participate, investigate, and help free the Lost Souls and defeat Candle Face. Still, finding the right balance between doing the work myself and handing off tasks has been difficult.

That's the core problem: how much should I rely on others, and how much should I rely on myself? It's been only 11 months since I started seeking help, but the paranormal community I've reached out to has been hesitant, scared, too busy, or not serious about the paranormal. Maybe it's time to rethink the plan and focus on sharpening my own abilities. If I truly have mediumship potential, then maybe I should explore that path more seriously. I've found an opportunity to do that.

This Saturday, September 28, 2024, a small gothic café and boutique called Triple Six Social in San Marcos, TX, is hosting a Mediumship Bootcamp. The description reads: "Unleash your inner mystic with our Mediumship Bootcamp, a powerful day intensive designed to sharpen your psychic abilities and deepen your connection with the spirit world." It sounds like a good fit for someone looking to sharpen those skills. But then I wonder: do I really need this? After all, the Lost Souls who come to me are clear as day, speaking directly to me without ghost boxes, Ouija boards, tarot cards, or crystal balls. While others in the paranormal community rely on those tools, I seem to access these communications without any aid. Lately, I've been experimenting with different ways of connecting to the Lost Souls, relying more on direct communication through visualization and deep meditation. I've noticed that I get clearer impressions when I shift my focus that way without needing external devices. It's not a perfect science, but it's a start. If I can refine this approach, maybe I won't need to rely on traditional methods at all. Maybe I should be teaching a class instead of attending one! Of course, I say this in jest, as there's always more to learn. I don't need these things, but continuing to learn never hurts.

On top of my mediumship abilities, I've been dabbling in remote viewing. I connected with a professional remote viewer named Stacey Tallitsch through the Get Haunted Network. He suggested that remote viewing might help me with the Lost Souls. Intrigued, I enrolled in his beginner's class. It's been fascinating but more challenging than I expected. For example, I discovered that what I see during remote viewing is often the opposite of reality, which is something I still struggle to adapt to. Maybe I need to modify the process to fit what I'm trying to do, just as I'm adjusting my mediumship abilities.

I even asked Stacey if he'd be willing to use his more advanced remote viewing skills to help with the Lost Souls, but I haven't received any help from him or other experts I've reached out to, just as I haven't received help from dream interpreters, psychics, and mediums. That's why I attended the Paranormal Fest 2024 at the Black Swan Inn: to try my luck with the Texas-based paranormal community. But here I am, back at square one, relying on myself and trying to sharpen my abilities while I waited for others to join in.

I've said this countless times before, but I still find myself drawn to the paranormal community, seeking assistance where none has been offered. I'll continue asking, but I must accept that help may remain hard to find. Maybe I'm meant to do most of this work myself while relying on my readers to support me with research and clues.

I'm beginning to realize that I may have to carry most of this work myself. Candle Face is closing in, and the Lost Souls are counting on me to hear their voices and make sure their stories are told. I'm determined. Determination without results won't bring them peace. And so far, I don't have many to show.

STRENGTHENING MY ABILITIES TO CONFRONT CANDLE FACE

October 2, 2024

Lately, I've been spending more time strengthening my remote viewing and mediumship abilities, both the ones I developed on my own and the new techniques I recently learned from Stacey Tallitsch's Remote Viewing class and Nicole Riccardo's Mediumship Bootcamp. It's been useful, and it's reinforced my belief that I can handle more of the paranormal side of my investigations myself and rely less on the paranormal community for assistance.

The Mediumship Bootcamp, led by Nicole Riccardo, introduced me to exercises designed to strengthen the different "clairs": clairvoyance (clear seeing), clairaudience (clear hearing), clairsentience (clear feeling), claircognizance (clear knowing), clairalience (clear smelling), and clairgustance (clear tasting). Each technique is meant to refine our intuitive senses, and I've blended these practices with my existing knowledge of remote viewing.

For example, Nicole says that one of the foundational exercises for developing clairvoyance involves meditating while looking into a flame or crystal ball. I have a large crystal ball that weighs over 20 pounds, which I originally bought as an office decoration back in my military intelligence days. Many Soldiers jokingly said that military intelligence personnel used crystal balls or witchcraft to predict or shape enemy operations, so it was my way of poking fun at that rumor. Still, I've found myself gazing at it while meditating, even though I said just days ago that I didn't need any aids. This practice is meant to train the mind's eye to receive images and gain clarity through visions. I've been adapting this technique by incorporating it into my remote viewing sessions. I stopped treating the scene as static and let my mind shift between different locations and events, pulling in visual information I might otherwise miss. This approach seems to be helping me connect with more details and visualize locations more deeply.

While I haven't seen anything concrete during these sessions, I do feel calmer and more relaxed. It feels like I'm settling into the practice, and I believe I'm heading in the right direction. The clarity will come with time, I hope.

The exercises to strengthen clairaudience, such as adjusting to background noises or isolating specific instruments in a song, are helping me refine my ability to distinguish between different voices or entities that might be trying to communicate with me. By isolating these sounds during remote viewing sessions, I can better interpret any auditory messages I receive instead of relying only on visual cues. It feels like tuning a radio dial, trying to find the frequency that lets me hear the spirits more clearly. During the Mediumship Bootcamp, Nicole played some of her own music, which featured six or seven different instruments. We were tasked with tuning into one instrument only. About halfway through the song, I found I could focus on that specific instrument, and I began to predict how the rest of the song would unfold. It felt strangely familiar even though I had never heard it before.

Another technique I'm working on is clairsentience, the ability to sense emotions and physical sensations. This has always been harder for me, as I tend to prioritize logic and reason over emotion. By practicing energy-sharing exercises, where one person sends an emotion and the other receives it, I'm becoming more aware of the emotional shifts during remote viewing sessions. I hope to eventually tap into the emotional states of the Lost Souls, giving me deeper context for the information they share. This practice is helping me understand the Lost Souls' emotions and get more comfortable working from my own emotions.

Working these techniques into my routine has been a step toward independence. I've always appreciated the information and support of psychics, mediums, and other members of the paranormal community. There have been times when I felt slowed down by the need to rely on others. Waiting for other people to confirm or interpret things often slowed my investigations. With remote viewing, the ability to project my consciousness to different locations and observe events has always been central to my work. Now, by combining it with these stronger intuitive abilities, I feel like I'm picking up details I wasn't getting before.

I also feel like I'm taking more control. I'm trusting myself more, even when the information isn't clear-cut. When a lost soul reaches out, or I sense Candle Face lurking nearby, I don't need to immediately turn to someone else for validation. I have the tools and confidence to explore these encounters on my own.

There'll always be a place for collaboration in this investigation, and I still value the views of trusted psychics, mediums, and paranormal investigators. By strengthening my own abilities, I'm hoping to fill in the gaps and approach my work with more self-reliance.

This shift in mindset has already started to work. The past few nights, the energy in my living room, where the spirits often manifest, feels different. Actually, I just thought of something: maybe I don't need to wait for the Lost Souls to come to me now, at least until I can sharpen my new skills. Maybe I can go directly to them. What if I could visit the sites where they were murdered and try to see what happened? I could put myself in the location, using my remote viewing and clairvoyance to pick up on any remaining energy, visual details, or even sounds that might have been left behind. This could provide location details, descriptions of the killers, and other key information such as terrain and weather conditions that day. Being physically present might help me connect more deeply and pick up information I couldn't perceive while sitting on my couch listening to the Lost Souls. It's a new approach, and I'm curious to see if it could help me find more clues. It also comes with risks. Physically visiting these locations could expose me to residual energy or encounters with entities still lingering at the sites, like Candle Face's shadows or Candle Face herself. Still, I'm willing to explore this option, keeping my guard up and preparing for anything. Am I starting to see things more clearly?

Looking at these new possibilities, it feels like I'm coming full circle. I began this mission with nothing but a strong desire to help these Lost Souls and find answers. Now, I'm learning how to carry more of this project myself, no matter where it leads. The classes were just the beginning. The real work is getting started. I feel more prepared and more committed than ever to helping these souls find peace.

A Personal Note to My Readers

I want to take a moment to thank all of you for being part of this mission with me. Dealing with Lost Souls and confronting Candle Face hasn't been easy, but your support and encouragement have helped. Every message I receive and every shared experience from those of you who have sensed or seen things paranormal reminds me that I'm not alone in this mission.

Your belief in my work has kept me motivated. As I continue to develop my own skills, maybe some of you will also look more closely at your own experiences and what may lie beyond. I'm grateful to have you with me.

I'd love to hear from you: Have any of you felt a similar shift in energy when practicing your own intuitive abilities? If so, what have you experienced? Please feel free to share in the comments or reach out to me directly.

Soon, I'll test some of these new ideas by visiting one of the sites mentioned by a lost soul. It's risky, but I believe it's worth trying. I'll document what happens.

I often wonder what keeps me going in the face of such evil. When I think about the Lost Souls and those rare moments when part of their story comes to the surface, I know why I keep going. They need help, and this project has changed me too. To each of you who reads these journal entries and supports my mission, thank you for being part of this story. We're in this together.

CANDLE FACE VICTIM #39: MARK'S ENDLESS JOURNEY

October 4, 2024

Last night, I did something different. I put aside Facebook and YouTube and decided to practice the mediumship techniques I've recently learned and combine them with remote viewing. I moved my crystal ball into the dining room and sat down to meditate and clear my mind. It was around 1:00 a.m., and I was the only one awake, but I still felt a little silly staring into a crystal ball. After a while, that feeling faded and was replaced by a sense of peace and mental clarity.

As I continued gazing into the crystal ball and focusing on my breathing, I heard the faint sound of footsteps approaching me from behind. I didn't turn around. I kept concentrating on the crystal ball because I somehow knew it was a lost soul. He sat down next to me and introduced himself as Mark. I finally looked up at him and saw a lost soul more clearly than ever before. The details in my dining room looked sharper too. I knew I was in some kind of trance, brought on by the meditation and the new techniques I'd been practicing.

He greeted me again with a look of amazement. He seemed amused that I was looking around the dining room, almost as if he couldn't believe I could see him. "Hello," he said again, trying to get my full attention. I finally looked directly at him, noticing that he had a much larger head than most and Spock-like, pointed ears. He was a white man, around 200 pounds, with blue eyes, and looked to be about 40 years old. He seemed to wait for me to take him in before speaking again.

"Hello," he said for the third time, laughing softly. "I walked here from Waco, nearly 175 miles, just to talk to you."

"You walked here from Waco?" I asked loudly.

"Yes," he chuckled. "I like to walk."

I knew I wasn't supposed to ask questions during these interactions because Candle Face forbids it. But I couldn't help myself. This felt too important. I decided to ask anyway.

"Why did you come all the way from Waco, Mark?"

His gaze turned more serious, his fingers tracing invisible patterns on the table. "Well, there's some folks down there who, uh, asked me to help them with something. They wanted me to hand out these pamphlets around town, y'know, spread the word about her."

"Pamphlets about Candle Face?" I asked.

"Yeah, yeah... We didn't call her Candle Face back then. I don't remember the name, though. The name had changed. The presence was Candle Face. I didn't believe in all that at first. Seemed like a buncha nonsense. I did it for the money. They didn't pay much, but it was somethin'. I ain't had much goin' for me, so I figured, why not? After a while, I dunno, it started to make more sense to me, y'know?" He paused, glancing down at his hands. "I kept talking to those folks, and it started feelin' real. So I got more excited 'bout helpin' 'em."

He hesitated before continuing. "They knew I was missin' a few marbles, though. I ain't exactly the sharpest tool in the shed. They kinda took advantage of that. Had me doin' stuff no one else wanted to do, and I didn't care. I was just happy to be part of somethin'. They was my new family."

Mark's expression brightened a little as he recalled the memory. "I really liked passin' out them pamphlets, long as I didn't have to talk to nobody. If folks started askin' questions, I'd just tell 'em, 'Read the pamphlet. It's all in there.' I wasn't good with answerin' questions, y'know?"

"What kind of things were in the pamphlet?" I asked, leaning forward slightly.

"Ah, just stuff 'bout Candle Face, or whatever her name is. How she's out there, helping her people and helping spread her message. The pamphlet made her seem like a god or something. My new friends would warn me not to cross her or she'd come after me too. I didn't think it was true at first. After a while, I started wonderin' if it was. I started gettin' real nervous handin' 'em out, like maybe she was watchin' me."

"Did you keep handing them out?"

He shook his head slowly. "Nah, I started feelin' weird 'bout it, like somethin' was wrong. So when I'd get more of 'em to pass out, I'd just walk. I like to walk, especially when I'm feelin' low. Walked way out in the countryside. Buried a bunch of them pamphlets in the dirt. Didn't wanna look at 'em no more." He glanced up at me, almost sheepish. "I'd still tell 'em I was handin' 'em out, though. Lied right to their faces."

"Why didn't you just quit?" I asked, even though I already sensed the answer.

Mark gave a small, sad smile. "Didn't wanna lose 'em. They was the only folks that ever cared about me. So I kept it up, kept walkin' 'round with those pamphlets. Then one day, I was walkin' along Highway 84, and a truck full of them saw me. Didn't have no pamphlets on me, just my own sorry self."

"What happened then?" I asked. I could tell the story was about to get worse.

"They pulled over. Said I was lettin' everybody down. Got real angry. I tried to say I'd do better, but they didn't listen." Mark looked down, touching his neck. "One of them pulled out a knife and stabbed me right here, right in the neck. Didn't even see it comin'. Then they dragged me off the road, into the brush. Left me there, bleedin' out. I felt my body go cold, heard the buzzards flappin' 'round. They picked at me 'til there wasn't much left."

I struggled to process what I'd just heard.

"That's why I walk," Mark said again, his voice growing softer. "Even after all that. I walk and I walk 'cause I ain't got nowhere else to go. And every place I go, it's like I'm seein' all the death and pain she's caused. People dead on the side of the road. Houses burned down. Folks screamin' for help that never comes."

He paused. "It's like I'm walkin' through Candle Face's own hell, a place she made just for me. My punishment for not handin' out those pamphlets. She made me see all this death and destruction. Things I coulda prevented if I'd done what I was supposed to. If I'd just passed out more pamphlets, maybe people woulda known about her. Maybe they wouldn't have died. Maybe they'd still be here." His voice was full of regret and guilt.

"That's my punishment. To walk forever in a place full of hurtin' people, a place I coulda stopped. She's showin' me what happens when folks don't know 'bout her. All because of me."

Mark's eyes stared through me, unfocused, as if he were no longer fully present in my dining room. His words tumbled out faster, almost frantic. "Every time I think I've walked far enough, I find myself right back where I started. I think I'm leavin' it all behind, and then there's more bodies, more pain. It's like she's watchin' me. Like she's laughin' at me."

I wanted to say something to ease his suffering, but I didn't know what.

"I'm so tired," Mark cried. "I just wanna rest. But I can't stop. I have to keep walkin'. Maybe if I walk long enough, she'll let me go. Maybe, just maybe, one day, I'll get outta here."

He glanced up at me, eyes full of desperate hope. "D'you think that's true? That if I keep goin', I'll find my way out? Or am I just stuck here forever?"

I tried not to show how much it got to me. "I don't know, Mark. I hope you do. I hope you find peace."

"Yeah, peace," he repeated softly, as if the word was foreign to him. "Peace would be nice."

Mark fell silent, staring off into the distance. Then, as if coming to a decision, he turned and started walking toward the door. I watched, helpless, as he moved with a slow, deliberate gait, like he was carrying the weight of the world on his shoulders. His form began to blur and fade as he stepped outside, but just before he disappeared completely, he glanced back over his shoulder.

"Thanks for talkin' to me," he said, his voice faint but sincere.

And then he was gone.

Personal Note to My Readers

Mark's story made me realize how important it is for me to refine my skills so I can connect with souls like Mark in a more meaningful way. Since completing Nicole Riccardo's Mediumship Bootcamp and Stacey Tallitsch's remote viewing class, I've been applying the meditation and focusing techniques they taught. I'm far from mastering these skills. Last night's encounter with Mark was the first time I really felt what this practice might lead to. The structured meditation exercises are starting to help me quiet my mind and filter out distractions. I'm noticing a difference, even if it's small.

One of the foundational exercises I learned from Nicole is grounding myself by visualizing roots extending from my feet into the earth. That has been particularly helpful in stabilizing my energy and maintaining focus. During my session with Mark, this grounding technique kept me centered as I felt his emotional turbulence wash over me. I could feel what he was carrying and still stay steady enough to understand his state of mind.

Another exercise I've incorporated is "target acquisition" from

Stacey's remote viewing course. Although I'm still getting the hang of it, I tried it with Mark. I focused on his voice and let my mind's eye follow it. This seemed to strengthen our connection and make his presence feel more solid. For a brief moment, I felt like I could see into his world more clearly.

I know it's just a start. These techniques are already making it easier to pick up on details that might have slipped past me before. I'm picking up more now. Mark's voice had texture and depth. I could hear it waver when he spoke about his past and steady itself when he asked whether I thought he could find peace. They're small shifts, and they tell me more than the words alone.

I haven't perfected these techniques overnight. I'm still trying to find the right balance between using them and letting these encounters happen naturally. Last night's experience with Mark showed me what may be possible if I keep working at this. For now, it's enough to know that I'm making progress and that these new techniques are helping me connect with them more clearly than before.

This feels like the start of something. I'm grateful to have you all along for the mission.

CANDLE FACE VICTIMS #40 AND #41: THE RANCHER AND HIS WIFE

October 6, 2024

The late-night Dallas Cowboys and Pittsburgh Steelers game had me all wound up, so I couldn't sleep. I lay down, but nothing. I tried counting sheep, reading a terms and conditions agreement word-for-word, and even watching a video on different types of rocks, but still nothing. Not even a hint of drowsiness. So I decided to sit up and do some breathing exercises to clear my mind. I figured since I couldn't sleep, I might as well try to call on a Lost Soul, even though I had never attempted to call one forward before. They come when they want to, not when summoned.

I had learned some basic mediumship techniques online, piecing together a method that seemed promising. After making a few adjustments to suit my style, I prepared myself for the session. First, I visualized a white light filling the room, a common protective measure recommended for these kinds of spiritual encounters. Next, I focused on deepening my breathing, counting to five on each inhale and exhale. With my eyes closed, I mentally projected an invitation, almost like throwing a lasso of energy into the void, and then waited, imagining that energy spreading out and drawing in anyone willing to communicate.

I'd read that summoning spirits could be dangerous, but I felt an odd sense of calm. Maybe it was because I didn't think it would actually work. Or maybe it was because, deep down, I wanted to see if I could do it.

After about ten minutes, the shadows in the living room began to darken, thickening like smoke, and the lights in the kitchen started flickering. Then, almost as if crossing a line, an old man stepped into my living room. He took a few cautious steps toward me, then stopped. He turned back to the shadow and made a beckoning motion, as if inviting someone to follow him.

An elderly woman then stepped out of the shadow and joined him. They both walked toward me, stopping when I scooted over to make room for them to sit.

"We're fine right here," the old man said in a slight Spanish accent, his voice steady but soft.

"How can I help y'all?" I asked, keeping my voice gentle.

"Ray, I want you to listen to our story. And only listen, take no action."

"OK," I responded. I wanted to ask why they wouldn't want me to take action, but I figured I'd understand as they spoke.

"We used to live in a small town east of Austin nearly 50 years ago. I'm originally from Mexico, but moved to Texas when I was a young man, around 20 years old. I made my money as a ranch hand until I saved enough to buy my own ranch and hire my own ranch hands. I remember living in Mexico and hearing stories of a once-beautiful little girl who was killed in a fire and now roams the earth looking to be remembered because people have forgotten her. My friends and I used to tell stories about her, probably adding things of our own, trying to one-up each other. After a while, we didn't know what was real and what wasn't. In the end, we all believed, and that's what counts."

"Is the little girl you're talking about Candle Face?" I asked.

"Yes," he answered in a matter-of-fact tone, as if I didn't even need to ask.

"Is Candle Face from Mexico?"

"You tell me, Mr. Investigator," he responded with a nasty tone, while the lady nudged him. "Be nice," she said.

"We're here to tell you about the circumstances of our deaths."

"OK, tell me whatever you want to tell me."

"I met my wife about 20 years after I settled in Texas from Mexico. She wasn't my first wife, and I have children from previous marriages. I talked a lot about my time in Mexico to my wife, especially stories about who you call Candle Face. At first, my wife didn't believe, but she came around. For the next few decades, things went well. We kept our faith in her, and she made sure our health was strong. We even talked to people in town about her loving ways, but most would just laugh. We were the crazies down the dirt road. Anyway, my wife started to lose her way and stopped talking about her. She didn't even want to listen to my stories anymore.

Eventually, my wife started to hear noises in her head, which turned into voices. These voices..."

I interrupted him and asked her to continue with the story.

She looked at me and smiled. "Thank you, Ray. At least someone lets me talk."

"These voices were incoherent. I never was able to understand them."

I saw this as a chance to use some remote viewing to "listen in" to these voices in her head at that time. I didn't think it would work, but I closed my eyes and focused on the memory of her hearing those voices. I imagined my consciousness slipping back in time, attaching itself to her presence as if I were standing beside her when it happened. As I looked deeper, I felt a faint ringing in my ears, like the low hum of static interference. Slowly, words began to filter through, a rambling chorus of overlapping screams.

"... why did you do it ... why did you leave her ... she's coming ... you can't run ... you're too weak ... she remembers ... it's your fault ... her eyes are burning ... you're the reason ... why didn't you stop her ... her face ... you're the reason she's like this ... end it with a knife ..."

The voices ran together into a rush of overlapping screams, each word echoing through my mind. I tried to make sense of them as the pressure built. It was as if dozens of voices were yelling directly into my brain, each one fighting to be heard over the others.

"You can't hide ... she's watching ... she'll make you see ... you'll see her face again ... forever ... it's all your fault ..."

I pulled myself back abruptly, gasping for air. The couple watched me, unblinking.

"She was trying to torment you," I said, my voice barely audible. "The voices were blaming you. They wanted you to suffer. They mentioned a knife. Did something happen in your home? Something involving a knife?"

The old man's eyes darkened, and he nodded slowly. His gaze fell to the floor. His wife remained silent.

"I killed her," he confessed softly, almost as if admitting it to himself for the first time. "Candle

Face was tormenting her, and I couldn't stand to see my wife suffer anymore. The voices wouldn't leave her alone. They kept saying terrible things. They were breaking her down, piece by piece."

"She begged me to help her," he continued, his voice trembling. "So I took my gun and shot her in our bedroom while she was standing next to the bathroom entrance. She didn't even scream, just looked at me with those haunted eyes, like she knew it was coming. She fell to the floor, and I barely had time to realize what I'd done before there was just a small pool of blood beneath her. I moved her body to my truck, cleaned the floor as best as I could, but the bathroom door had a hole in it that I couldn't fix. That type of door isn't manufactured anymore. So I took it off its hinges and hid it in the barn under a pile of old hay. My plan was to burn her body, then bury the bones somewhere in South Texas and move back to Mexico. But before I could..."

The old woman's hand tightened on his arm, as if bracing him for what came next.

"My son showed up," the old man said. "It was an unannounced visit. Came out of nowhere. He didn't know what I'd done to his stepmother. Didn't even suspect it. He saw me outside, standing by my truck, and he must have seen something in my face, or maybe it was just bad timing. It was like he was being pulled there by something else, something I couldn't see."

His voice dropped lower, trembling as he continued. "He got real angry, like something snapped in him. He accused me of trying to sell off the ranch or leave him behind. I tried to calm him down, but he wouldn't listen. One moment he was yelling, and the next, he pulled out a gun. He shot me, right there beside the truck. Cold, like it didn't mean a thing. I remember falling, staring up at the sky, wondering if this was how it all ended. He didn't even check if I was dead. Just grabbed my body and tossed it into the back of the truck in a hurry."

His wife's eyes were fixed on the floor.

"He was in such a rush, he didn't notice her," the old man continued, his gaze shifting to his wife. "My wife's body was already in the truck bed, wrapped up in an old tarp. He didn't even know she was there, didn't know I'd killed her to end her suffering. He just threw me in with her remains and drove off, leaving the blood in the dirt outside the house. He drove all the way to South Texas and buried us deep in the desert, like we were nothing. Then he just left. I guess he carried out my plan for me."

His voice trembled. "He buried his own father and stepmother. All because of a misunderstanding, because of a moment of anger. And now he thinks I was going to abandon him, that I was going to run away."

The old woman's hand tightened around her husband's arm. "He doesn't know the truth," she said, her voice strained. "And we can never tell him. You can never tell him. He did what he thought he had to do. We don't want him to get in trouble. He's already paid enough."

The old man nodded slowly. "We don't blame him, Ray. He didn't know. And now we're stuck here, trapped in this cycle, because Candle Face won't let us go. She wants us to relive it all, the regret, the pain, over and over again."

He looked up suddenly, a flicker of memory in his eyes. "Just before he shot me, I swear I heard Candle Face yell in my ear, 'This is your reward,' like she was smiling at what was about to happen."

A son, unwittingly burying his parents in a fit of rage, believing he was left behind. A husband who took his wife's life to spare her agony, only to find himself punished for it in death.

They looked at me, eyes hollow but pleading. "Just don't let anyone come after him," the old man pleaded. "He's been through enough already. Please."

The couple's forms dissolved, their outlines blurring and fading.

I knew there was no way to ease their pain or undo Candle Face's torment. Something else bothered me too. This didn't feel like a random encounter. Candle Face had allowed them to come to me. She made sure I heard every detail of their story. Why?

I kept replaying their words, the fear and anguish in every line. Candle Face didn't want me to simply hear it. She wanted me to remember it. She was directing something I still couldn't fully see, making sure I became part of whatever she was doing.

My heart hammered against my ribs as I stood up, my legs trembling beneath me. The shadows lengthened at the corners of my vision. Candle Face was using their torment to work on me.

She wanted me to feel the same helplessness she forces on her victims. It didn't matter how many spirits came to me, how many stories I listened to. I couldn't change what happened to them. That was the feeling she wanted to leave me with.

A sharp sizzling sensation hit me in the chest, and I knew without a doubt her attention had shifted toward me as well.

Every word they spoke felt like part of something she wanted me to piece together. The more I know, the deeper I may be getting into whatever she's building around me. Whatever game she was playing, she had just pulled me further into it. My hands shook as I clenched them into fists.

I had a sinking feeling that more stories like this one were on their way. More souls, more pain, and with each one Candle Face would be there, watching what it did to me.

This wasn't over.

As I glanced around my living room, I felt her presence curling around me like smoke, a faint, mocking laughter bouncing off the walls. I knew Candle Face was smiling.

Because she knew she had me exactly where she wanted me.

Personal Note to My Readers (Updated on Oct 8, 2024)

I've been doing a lot of thinking after this last encounter. Every time a lost soul reaches out to me, sharing their pain and tragedy, I'm left wondering if I'm really helping them or just playing into Candle Face's hands. The more I look at it, the more I see her using these souls to work on me. To make me feel their suffering, the frustration of not being able to do anything to change their fate, and that crushing sense of powerlessness.

Just because Candle Face thinks she's pulling the strings doesn't mean I'm going to stop trying to help. Simply acknowledging the pain these souls have gone through is still a way of pushing back. I'm giving them a voice, even if Candle Face wants me to think it's pointless. That's probably why she's so determined to keep twisting things around.

She wants me to believe that I'm just a helpless observer, that no matter what I do, it won't matter. That's her game. Make me doubt myself. Make me think I'm as trapped as these souls. But I'm not giving in. Every time I listen to these stories and share them, I'm pushing back against her control, even if it's only a little. I know she's using this confusion and these stories to weaken my determination, but I'm not giving in.

Take, for example, the voices the old woman heard during our encounter. The words were Candle Face's twisted way of breaking her spirit. The voices kept harping on things that made no sense, feeding on her guilt, confusion, and fear. That's the thing. None of it is meant to make sense. It's meant to drive her mad and leave her questioning everything.

And if the voices didn't make sense to you either, that's because they weren't supposed to. That's Candle Face's tactic: keep it chaotic, keep it disturbing, and keep it personal. Let me break it down for you line by line:

- "… why did you do it …" It's like Candle Face was trying to make the woman doubt herself, planting the idea that she did something wrong even if she didn't. That vague accusation stays, making it impossible for her to feel peace.

- "… why did you leave her …" Who's "her"? Candle Face? Someone else? It's designed to poke at the woman's guilt, make her think she abandoned or betrayed someone. When you start doubting yourself, it's easy to spiral into regret.

- "… she's coming … you can't run …" This is a scare tactic. It's meant to raise her anxiety and fear, making her feel trapped and powerless.

- "… you're too weak …" Candle Face is attacking her sense of self here, breaking down whatever confidence she had left. She wants her to feel powerless against what's happening to her.

- "… she remembers … it's your fault …" This is Candle Face planting a false story, making the woman believe that something she did or didn't do is the reason all this is happening. It doesn't have to be true, just convincing enough to create more doubt and guilt.

- "… her eyes are burning …" A reference to Candle Face's appearance. It's meant to force the woman to relive that face and the fear that comes with it.

- "… you're the reason … why didn't you stop her …" Candle Face is making her feel responsible for something she never had any control over. She's twisting the truth into something that feeds on regret.

- "… her face … you're the reason she's like this …" It's a direct accusation, making it personal. Candle Face wants the woman to think she's to blame for everything Candle Face has become. Whether it's true or not doesn't matter. It's meant to hurt.

But the part that really threw me off was when the voices started mentioning a knife. I know the husband killed his wife with a gun, so why bring up a knife? It doesn't add up. And I've been thinking about that for a while now.

I think Candle Face throws in false details like that to confuse and disorient her victims even more. Maybe she wants them to think they're forgetting something, or worse, remembering something that never happened. That's another way to make them question their own sanity, to make them feel like they're losing touch with reality. And in a way, that may be the worst part of it. You start to think, "What if I've forgotten something terrible?" or "What if I'm not remembering things correctly?" That knife didn't exist, but in the old woman's mind, it's now part of her story, another burden she has to carry.

There is another part of their account that I can't ignore. The old man said his son didn't know his stepmother's remains were already in the truck when he threw his father's body in. That may explain the first mistake. It doesn't fully explain the burial in South Texas. If the son removed his father from the truck himself, he should have had some chance of seeing that someone else was already there. One possible explanation is that the old man was already dead by that point and knew only that he had been thrown into the truck, not what his son saw afterward. Another is that Candle Face had already begun doing what she does so often in these cases: clouding memory, distorting sequence, and leaving her victims with gaps they can't close. For now, I'm treating that part of the testimony as unsolved.

That's how Candle Face works: by turning truth into lies, mixing up memories, and making you feel responsible for things you never did. The real damage is what she does to the mind.

She wants her victims confused, torn apart by doubt, and constantly questioning their own reality. The voices are there to blur the line between truth and fiction, making the woman feel guilty for things that never even happened. That's how she breaks them.

But here's where I stand: every encounter with the Lost Souls, every technique I strengthen, gives me a clearer picture of Candle Face's tactics. I'm learning how to sort through the chaos.

I know she wants me to feel trapped, just like she did with that couple. She wants me to believe I'm just another pawn in her sick game. But I'm not backing down. I'm going to keep listening to these Lost Souls, keep sharing their stories, and keep pushing back against whatever twisted game she's playing.

It's not over. I refuse to be just another pawn on her board. I'll keep fighting for these souls, no matter how hard she makes me doubt myself.

I'm not going anywhere.

CANDLE FACE VICTIM #42: THE CROWN OF BONE

October 10, 2024

I've had some success with my newfound mediumship and remote viewing skills lately. Just a few days ago, I was able to 'hear' voices in an elderly woman's head from more than 50 years ago. It's a start. For example, I heard the voices mention a knife, even though a gun killed her. Did I not hear it correctly, or was I interpreting it wrong? For now, I believe I heard the word "knife," though I wonder if the voices were lying to me, or at least trying to manipulate me. I don't know yet. Hopefully, I can figure it out. I sure wish I had some brave and trustworthy psychics and mediums out there who could help me. I feel all alone in this investigation.

I hope I can enlist readers to help, though competing for their attention is hard work. Millions of books and websites are out there, all trying to grab their share of the audience. I'm one person on an important mission to find the right readers, readers who can help solve these cases and aid the Lost Souls.

Sorry, I digressed.

The lights flickered as I sat at the dining room table, pondering these thoughts while staring deep into the crystal ball around 2:00 a.m. Flickering lights seem to be the norm these days, a sign that Lost Souls are about to visit. I was right. I felt a couple of pokes on the back of my right shoulder. I jumped a little, despite knowing what was happening. I turned to my right, but nothing was there. Then I turned to my left, and before I could really see anything, two hands grabbed my shoulders and shook me hard. I heard a loud "Boo!"

I turned further around and saw a young black woman, probably around 25 years old, standing slightly behind me, laughing.

"I always wanted to do that," she said, still chuckling. "That's what ghosts are supposed to do, right?"

"I guess," I said, half-laughing, trying to hide that she had actually startled me.

She pulled out the chair next to me and sat down. She seemed completely at ease, as if she'd done this before, or at least like she was comfortable with me. She had a nice smile and bright teeth, but her skin looked as though it had been drained of all color, with a faint bluish tint. Her eyes, though, were full of laughter.

But what stood out most was that she had been completely scalped. Not a patch of hair or skin on her head, just exposed skull, with blood still flowing down her face. Her yellow shirt was almost completely soaked in blood.

"What do you think of my hairstyle?" she asked, pretending to comb through non-existent hair.

"I like it," I said, trying to remain calm.

She laughed, clearly picking up on my discomfort.

"I'm here to ask you to help me find my body and figure out how I was killed. I was too high on drugs the day it happened, so I don't remember much. The word in Candle Face's Lair is that you can see the past."

She stressed the words "The word in Candle Face's Lair," almost mockingly.

Before she could say anything else, I interrupted. "No, I can't do that. I've been practicing, but I can't do it for real yet."

"But Ray, you must try. Look into your crystal ball and do your thing."

Reluctantly, I looked down into the crystal ball. I felt like I was being put on the spot, asked to try something I wasn't even sure I could do. Her big smile had faded into a sad frown. I think I saw tears mixed with the blood running down her face. Now, I had to try.

"As a matter of fact," she added, "today is the anniversary of my death. That's why I'm here. My birthday was just a few days ago, and now this."

"I'm so sorry. Celebrating a birthday, then dying a few days later. Happy birthday," I said.

"Thank you," she said, but her focus stayed on my crystal ball.

She watched me intently as I sat there with the crystal ball. My hands hovered over the ball, feeling a faint warmth, though I knew it was just my nerves. I put my hands down, thinking I must look ridiculous, like I was in some movie, acting out a scene.

I stared deep into the crystal ball, focusing on the energy around me, trying to connect with whatever traces of her past still remained. I followed standard remote viewing practices: grounding myself, clearing my mind, and letting the sensations and images come naturally. In mediumship, you open yourself to the spirit's energy, allowing it to guide you to the memories or traces it leaves behind. The key is to trust that what you see, no matter how broken, means something.

The flickering lights in the kitchen slowed, and for a moment, the dining room fell into a creepy calm. I began to see flashes, not in the crystal ball, but in my mind: scattered images, unclear but connected to her story. A park bench, the flash of metal, muffled voices. Nothing was clear. One thing was certain: this was no simple death. Whoever did this didn't want her found.

"I see something," I began. "It's not clear. It feels like you were in a public place, maybe a park."

She nodded slightly. "That sounds right. But who? Why?"

"I'm not sure yet. I'll keep trying," I said. "This isn't easy to piece together, but I'll do what I can."

Her expression softened, and for a moment, I could see that behind the blood and pain, there was still hope in her.

Before I could say another word, the room grew hot. So hot it felt like the sun's surface, right in my dining room. I turned, and there she was, Candle Face. Her charred features looked darker than usual, and her hollow eye sockets glowed faintly as if the fire within her still burned.

The lost soul beside me looked terrified, her hands trembling. Candle Face's eyes locked onto the woman's forehead.

"What happened to you?" Candle Face asked in a low, mocking voice. "Looks like you have been scalped."

She circled the dining room table slowly, like a predator toying with its prey.

The woman didn't answer, frozen.

Without warning, Candle Face pulled a knife from her cloak, its blade gleaming in the dim light. She leaned in, tracing an old scar just below the woman's exposed skull with the tip of the blade. The woman whimpered, her eyes wide with terror, unable to move.

"You know what is funny?" Candle Face asked. "You came here to ask Ray what happened to you? I can tell you. I was the one who scalped you. It was not enough, was it?"

She moved swiftly, and in one motion, she scalped the woman again, this time taking the top of her skull off and exposing the brain. Blood gushed as Candle Face held the bloody top of the skull in her hands, inspecting it as if it were a trophy.

The woman screamed in pain as her brain was exposed.

"She thought she could betray me," Candle Face scoffed while facing me. "She dared to speak my name, to reveal my secret, thinking she could escape. But no one escapes me."

I watched in disbelief as Candle Face took the woman's skull and placed it atop her own head like a grisly crown, the woman's blood now dripping down Candle Face's face but boiling away within seconds.

"This," she said with a twisted smile, "is what happens when you speak my name to non-believers."

And that's when it hit me. This woman was killed because she had learned the truth about Candle Face. She had tried to warn others, and Candle Face got to her first. Her death was a message: Candle Face's secrets were not to be exposed.

The lost soul disappeared, and Candle Face remained with her new crown.

She returned her gaze to me, her hollow eye sockets narrowing.

"So," she scoffed, "you think you are getting better at this little 'mediumship' act of yours? How adorable."

She paced around the dining room. "You think you can peek into my past? You think you are the first to try?"

She paused, leaning in so close I could feel the heat radiating from her charred skin. "That woman thought the same thing," she said, gesturing to where the lost soul had sat moments before. "She thought she could use her 'abilities' to fight me too, to dig into secrets that do not belong to her. And look what it got her: scalped, mutilated, and now a crown for me."

Candle Face ran her fingers across her new crown, smirking as she adjusted it on her head. "You see, Ray, my past is not for the likes of you. It is for my children. Non-believers, you saw what happened to them. My children know what to tell and what not to tell."

"You could end up just like her," she yelled, her voice hotter. "Scalped, gutted, and left for dead. You are playing with fire, Ray. Look into my past, and I promise you will burn."

I clenched my fists under the table, forcing myself to stay calm. "I've heard these empty threats from you before," I said, my voice firm. "Here I am, still here."

Her smile faded, replaced by a look of fury. "You think you are safe? You think you are untouchable. You are wrong, Ray. So very wrong. I have not killed you yet because you are my ultimate prize. Do you have any idea how long I have waited for this? How long I have wanted to rip you apart, piece by piece, until there is no memory of your existence?"

She circled the table again, slower this time, her footsteps echoing in the quiet room. "I am patient," she continued. "Oh, I am so patient. And when the time comes, when you finally slip, I will be there. I will be the last thing you see, Ray. And I will enjoy every second of it."

For a moment, neither of us spoke. The tension between us thickened.

"You want to know why no one from the paranormal community wants to help you?" she asked, breaking the silence. "It is because of me. They know what I can do. They have seen it. That is why they stay away. They know my power and are smart enough to keep their distance."

She leaned in again, her face inches from mine. "You should be wary of your little 'abilities,' Ray. Keep looking into my past, and you may not like what you find. It is not just the Lost Souls you are dealing with. You are in my world, and in my world, the rules are different."

I stared back at her. "Is that all you've got?" I asked, raising an eyebrow. "More threats? More warnings? You've tried to scare me before, and guess what? I'm still here. I've fought bigger demons than you."

Her hollow eye sockets flashed with anger. "Bigger demons?" she spat. "You have no idea what I am, Ray. You will. Soon enough, you will."

For a moment, I thought she might attack. Her body tensed, her hand gripping the knife tightly. Then she straightened up, a strange smile creeping across her face.

"You know," she said, her tone almost casual, "you are not as far along in your mediumship as you think you are. You are tapping into something much darker, much deeper than you realize. And that little crystal ball of yours? It is a window. You look through it, and I look through it too."

I blinked, caught off guard. "What do you mean?"

She laughed again, that same mocking sound. "Oh, you will find out soon enough. Keep using your abilities. Keep pushing yourself. The more you try to see into my past, the closer you bring me to you. Every time you look, every time you connect with one of my victims, you open the door a little wider. And one day, I will step through for the last time and take you with me."

She took a step back, her eyes gleaming with twisted delight. "So keep practicing, Ray. Keep looking. Just remember, whatever you are staring at is staring back at you."

With that, she turned and walked toward the shadowy corner of the room. Just before disappearing, she paused and looked over her shoulder. "I will be seeing you soon."

And then she was gone.

As terrifying as Candle Face is, I can't get rid of the feeling that I'm not alone in this fight. She's powerful, and I still believe there's strength in numbers, in collaboration. The paranormal community has faced evil before, and together, along with my readers, we might just stand a chance against her. If there are brave souls out there who still believe in fighting for what's right, I welcome your help. This battle belongs to all of us.

Personal Note to My Readers

I sat there for a moment, my mind racing. What had she meant? A window for her too? Was it possible that my mediumship and remote viewing were somehow connected to her, that I was giving her more power by using my abilities? This would explain why I can't seem to see beyond her victims. Could Candle Face, the shadows, and even the Lost Souls be watching me through the crystal ball? Is that how they know my every move?

Once again, I felt like I had failed. I wanted to help, and I hurt another lost soul instead. Her trust in me was misplaced, and I worry that my attempts are doing more harm than good. How can I protect these Lost Souls when I can't even find their remains? To date, I've only identified 6 of 42 Lost Souls. Maybe I need to focus more on how to protect them than on trying to identify them. I must find a way to shield them from Candle Face, even if I can't yet give them the peace they seek.

Here I am again, swinging between hope and hopelessness. Every time I feel like I'm making progress, Candle Face rips it away from me. She shatters every flicker of hope and leaves me feeling more helpless than before. It's exhausting. Every time I think I'm getting somewhere, she drags me back into a great depression. I can't keep up with the emotional whiplash anymore.

I've been here before. I've wondered if I'm making a difference or just playing into her hands. Am I really helping these souls, or am I just another pawn in her twisted game? Am I in her hell, just like her victims, being tortured slowly, methodically, before she takes me too?

Then something in me shifted tonight. I surprised myself. My fists were clenched under the table, steady against my legs as they used to be when Candle Face visited me as a child. Back then, I was frozen in fear, unable to move, barely able to breathe when she came near. Tonight, I stood up to her, or at least I tried to.

I can't believe I told Candle Face that I've fought bigger demons than her. Of course, that's not true. I've never faced anything like her in my life. Maybe I said it out of fear, trying to sound tough. Maybe I said it because, deep down, I needed to convince myself that I can beat her. I don't know. I said it, and I still can't believe those words came out of my mouth. Kind of funny, though.

I don't know if I can win this battle. I can't give up on these Lost Souls, no matter how many times Candle Face tries to break me. I have to keep fighting, for them, for the truth, for something bigger than my own survival.

I might be in her hell, being tortured just like her victims before she takes them. I'm not ready to give in. Not yet. Candle Face can threaten me all she wants. I've seen what she does, and I'm still here. There must be a reason why I'm still here.

I know Candle Face wants me to feel isolated, to think I'm in this alone. I don't believe that. I've always trusted in the power of collaboration. She's strong. I know there are others out there in the paranormal community and among my readers who are just as strong, even though I know I must carry the bulk of the work. I welcome any help. Together, I believe we can free these Lost Souls, no matter how powerful Candle Face thinks she is.

I have to keep going. One way or another.

IS CANDLE FACE USING MY CRYSTAL BALL?

October 14, 2024

It's been gnawing at me for days now. I keep thinking the crystal ball in the back of my home office isn't just a tool for me. Could Candle Face be using it to spy on me, to watch my every move, and decide which lost soul she'll send next? It sounds absurd at first, but thinking it through, it makes more sense than I'd like to admit. Too many times, a lost soul has appeared just as I've been making a critical decision, as though Candle Face knew exactly what I was thinking and sent them at just the right moment.

For example, back in December 2023, a paranormal investigative team reached out to me, saying they wanted to help me with Candle Face. I was excited. Finally, a team that showed bravery instead of the cowardice I had grown used to. We spoke for about an hour over a video chat, where I explained Candle Face's lore and shared some of the visions I've been having. But as the conversation went on, I realized they treated the work like a comedy routine, poking fun at the very things they claimed to want to help with. A few days later, after thinking it over, I turned down their help. The Lost Souls want answers, not a late-night comedy show.

What's interesting is what happened next. Just a few hours after that video chat ended, the eighth lost soul visited me, a woman who had been a paranormal investigator herself. She warned me not to allow any kind of mockery in my investigations, especially with the paranormal team I had just spoken to. She told me Candle Face doesn't like being mocked. Could she have been watching the video chat through the crystal ball? Or was it Candle Face, using the crystal ball to monitor everything and then sending the lost soul to deliver the warning?

I've been wondering whether I should keep using the crystal ball at all. If it's become a link for Candle Face to infiltrate my home, do I really want to keep it around? Maybe I should move it to a different room, out of sight, out of mind. But what if that's not enough? What if Candle Face can still use it, no matter where I put it?

Another thought keeps crossing my mind. Should I destroy it? Smashing it could sever that connection once and for all, or it could leave me even more vulnerable. There's a chance destroying the ball could anger her or, worse, leave me exposed without the one tool that's helped me reach out to the Lost Souls in the first place. What if the ball is also a protective layer between me and whatever else is out there?

Maybe I should try something else. Could it be possible to cleanse the crystal ball somehow, purging Candle Face's power over it? Maybe a ritual or even advice from a spiritual leader could help.

I don't know what the answer is yet, but I need to make a decision soon. Each time I sit down in my office, I can't help but feel watched.

The question is, watched by whom?

IDENTIFIED? – CANDLE FACE VICTIM #42: THE CROWN OF BONE

October 17, 2024

I keep wrestling with the same painful question: how can I help the Lost Souls if I can't identify them? This conflict feels sharper after a previous encounter, when the family and friends of another lost soul reached out and asked me to stop mentioning their loved one on my podcast. I ended the podcast out of respect for their wishes, yet the dilemma remains. And now, when a spirit like Victim #42 reaches out, full of hope and sadness, it feels as though she believes I'm her last chance. How can I honor both requests: the living who need peace, and the dead who need a voice?

In her testimony a few nights ago, the spirit revealed that October 10 was the anniversary of her death and that her birthday had been a few days earlier. Dates like these are invaluable clues, critical markers that can link to missing persons reports or trace timelines, offering clues to identities that might otherwise remain hidden. Knowing this, I began searching for any missing persons who disappeared in Central Texas on October 10 and whose birthday was shortly before she went missing. It was a long shot, but the urgency in her voice and the importance of those dates left me no choice. Google led me to a very similar listing on TheDoeNetwork, one about a woman who disappeared on October 10, 1992, with a birthday of October 7, 1967. The report even noted that she was last seen wearing a yellow shirt and had a scar "in the scalp area on her forehead," an uncanny match to the spirit's description.

It felt like she had been waiting for someone to make the connection. But can I be certain? Even if this spirit is the woman I found in that report, how can I pursue this without betraying her family's need for peace? The spirits want to be known, but I want to protect the families they left behind.

I think of what it would be like to show up on this woman's family's doorstep and say, "Your loved one came to me one night, asking for help." Then how would I even begin to explain that she's missing half of her skull? I'd be seen as a cruel stranger dredging up old wounds, and the family might look at me with horror, questioning my sanity. But the pain in that spirit's eyes was unmistakable. She trusts me to help her. So how do I honor that trust without betraying her family's need for peace?

I can't turn my back on the Lost Souls who come to me, now that my abilities are growing. But every time I think I'm making progress, I'm dragged back into the same helplessness. How can I help her if I'm stuck here, balancing between helping the dead and protecting the living?

I question whether I'm really prepared for this investigation. Yes, my skills are improving. I've reached a point I once only dreamed of. But for what? To be bound by the same restrictions I had before, forever torn between protecting the families and my duty to the Lost Souls. I see now that I can identify them if I try hard enough. Yet where does that leave me? Just as desperate as before, only now I know who they are, and I know that I can't do anything with that knowledge.

I don't know what to do, but I do know one thing: if that spirit truly is who I think she might be, I won't give up. I can't promise that I won't struggle or stumble along the way, but I won't stop trying to find a way to help her and all the others who wait in line to speak to me. I may be caught between two worlds, but if there's even the slightest chance I can free her without causing more harm, I'll find it.

But tonight, as I sit here, I feel more alone than ever.

Personal Note to My Readers

As I write this, I find myself struggling with a difficult decision. I believe I may have a name for this lost soul. But as you may have noticed, I haven't shared her name. I keep circling back to the question: should I? Should I include her name, bringing her closer to the peace she seeks, or should I protect the families she left behind? I'd like to ask you: what do you think? Is helping the Lost Souls more important than respecting the wishes of the living? Or are the living, with their fragile balance between healing and memory, more deserving of protection?

When a lost soul comes to me, I'm faced with their suffering, their longing to be known, and their desperation to reach someone who can listen and understand. They're no longer part of our world, yet their connection to it remains powerful through me. The living, however, carry the grief, often silently. To honor both sides of this mission, to give peace to the dead without harming the living, feels like an impossible line to walk.

If I share a name, it could reopen wounds, but if I don't, I'm leaving a lost soul adrift, missing a piece of their story. It's a question I wrestle with daily, and I'm not sure I'll ever fully answer. I appreciate any thoughts or guidance you can share on this subject. I'm grateful to have each of you beside me in this mission.

CANDLE FACE VICTIM #43 PUSHED FROM CONGRESS AVENUE BRIDGE

October 24, 2024

I used the crystal ball again just after midnight to call on a lost soul. My attempt with Candle Face Victim #42 had succeeded, so why not try again?

I took the crystal ball from my home office and placed it on the dining room table, just as I had before. I settled into the silence, took a deep breath, and tried to tap into the mediumship and remote viewing skills I've been honing. I recalled the session with Victim #42, the clear but desperate cries as Candle Face scalped her. Would this attempt bring the same clarity, or was I about to open myself up to Candle Face's gaze again?

The crystal's surface slowly clouded, pulling me into a scene. I recognized the location immediately: Congress Avenue in downtown Austin, overlooking Town Lake. My perspective felt detached, as if I were watching from a third-person perspective. Four figures stood on the bridge.

A young man, likely in his late twenties, struggled at the edge of the bridge, pleading with his attackers. His voice, thick with fear, cracked as he begged for his life. "Please, don't do it. I'll do anything, please!" The desperation in his words rang in my ears as if I were truly there, witnessing his final moments.

I studied the attackers, taking in each detail so I could capture them in my journal. The first was a tall man, around six feet, muscular but lean. His hooded jacket obscured part of his face, but his strong jawline and piercing eyes stood out. His grip on the victim's shoulder was firm, as if he had no doubt about what was coming.

Beside him stood a woman, likely in her mid-twenties, perhaps 5'5", her frame abnormally thin. Her hair was pulled back. A fitted black leather jacket hugged her form, and she watched the victim's pleas with a disturbing calmness.

The third attacker was another man, around 5'10", and heavier-set. His dark jeans and worn flannel shirt looked rough, adding to his unkempt appearance. Unlike the others, his eyes darted around, as if searching for someone or something.

Then they moved together, forcing the man over the bridge's edge, his cries cut off in a final scream. I could almost feel his terror, the shock, and the horrifying finality as his body plummeted, the water below breaking his fall with a distant splash.

The three attackers didn't stay. They fled up Congress Avenue, their footsteps slapping against the pavement, before turning east onto 1st Street and vanishing around the corner.

I blinked back into the dining room as the scene faded from the crystal ball. I got the clarity I wanted. It left me with another question: had Candle Face been watching too? Was she guiding me to these visions, feeding me memories she wanted me to see?

About ten minutes later, as I sat in my home office typing up the vision for my Candle Face Chronicles journal, I heard a noise coming from the living room. I knew what it was. I sat there, staring at the screen, waiting for a lost soul to arrive. Thirty seconds passed, and then, slowly, a figure emerged and walked into my office.

Dripping wet, the young man I had just seen in the vision walked toward me, his eyes wide and disoriented. Water pooled beneath him as he stood there trembling. His stare locked onto mine, and he spoke in a fearful, urgent voice.

"Look into the crystal ball again," he said frantically, his voice breaking. He paused as if struggling to get out more words but could only repeat, "Look into the crystal ball."

Hesitantly, I returned to the crystal ball on the dining room table, the room silent except for the faint dripping of water from the spirit behind me. I reached out, my fingers brushing against the cold surface, and peered into it.

At first, nothing but emptiness filled the crystal ball. Then, slowly, a figure took shape. A gaunt face with charred, hollowed eyes stared back at me. It was Candle Face.

She appeared as if deep inside the crystal's core, her burned, twisted features pressed against the glass, as though waiting to be unleashed. Her eye sockets glowed faintly, her mouth curving into an evil smile, and though she didn't speak, the hatred was unmistakable.

Suddenly, the crystal ball grew unbearably hot, steam creeping along its surface. I gasped, instinctively jerking my hand away. In an instant, Candle Face's image vanished.

Turning back, I saw that the man's figure had disappeared, leaving only faint puddles where he had stood moments before. I was alone in the room again, left with the sense that Candle Face was watching me and using these visions to control me. The young man's plea still plays in my mind: "Look into the crystal ball."

Personal Note to My Readers

A young man was forced over the edge of a bridge, pleading for mercy, and I watched every second of it. And just when I thought the encounter had ended, he appeared in my home, dripping wet. What rattled me most was his desperate request: "Look into the crystal ball again." When I did, I saw Candle Face, her twisted face pressed against the glass, watching, mocking, waiting.

I keep wondering what the purpose of this vision was. Why did the spirit urge me to look into the crystal ball, knowing it would reveal Candle Face herself?

He seemed terrified, as though warning me was as urgent as his last moments on that bridge. Was he simply seeking help, or was he warning me about the crystal ball? Did he know what Candle Face wanted to show me? These questions raise more possibilities. Was he compelled by Candle Face herself to lead me to her image, to draw me closer to her? The crystal ball feels tied to spirit communication, and it may also be a portal Candle Face is using to manipulate the Lost Souls and me.

Should I stop using the crystal ball altogether, as I mentioned before? The image of Candle Face pressed against it, as if inside, waiting to pounce on me, tells me she's somehow tied to it. But is that reason enough to destroy it? If I do, will I lose my connection to the Lost Souls, or will I be closing off Candle Face's entry into my world? Perhaps this vision, and Candle Face's message within it, was meant as a warning that while I'm helping the Lost Souls, I may also be feeding her power. She may be taunting me, showing me she has a hold on me through the crystal ball, like a spider weaving me into her web strand by strand.

Destroying the crystal ball might cut that connection. It might also silence the voices of the Lost Souls who still seek me out. It's a dilemma. If I keep it, I risk Candle Face getting me eventually. If I destroy it, I risk losing a vital tool for helping the spirits who are desperately seeking my aid. Or maybe the crystal ball has nothing to do with any of this. After all, I was communicating with the Lost Souls before using it.

For now, I'll leave the crystal ball untouched and watch it closely. This experience has shown me that Candle Face isn't content to stay on the sidelines. She's reminding me that she's watching, and that each vision may reveal something while also setting a trap. If she truly is using the crystal ball as a conduit, I may need to prepare for a future without it and find new ways to reach and help the Lost Souls, ways Candle Face can't control.

In the meantime, I'll continue to write down every encounter, every vision, every warning. I'll remain vigilant, watching Candle Face as closely as she watches me.

UNCLEAR FIGURES IN THE CRYSTAL BALL

October 27, 2024

Today, I spent some time with the crystal ball, practicing during the day. Working in daylight feels different, less intense than my usual nighttime sessions, which makes it easier to focus on technique without getting caught up in the energy around it. My goal was to see what, if anything, would come through on its own, without reaching out to the Lost Souls.

After a few minutes, shapes began to emerge in the crystal ball. At first, they were just shadows, faint and shifting, until they settled into a scene that felt somewhat familiar. It looked like a dark, enclosed space, with sloped walls and rough wooden beams faintly visible in the background. The ceiling seemed high in some places and low in others.

A layer of dust hung in the air, catching what little light there was and reflecting it into the crystal ball.

Scattered through the space were a few shadowed figures, some standing against the slanted boards, others sitting or crouched in the darker corners. They were all still, either looking down or straight ahead, as though waiting. I tried to focus on their faces, hoping for even a hint of a feature that might reveal more, but everything stayed blurred. Their faces shifted or faded each time I thought I'd caught a glimpse of an eye or a mouth.

As I continued to look, I realized that none of them were moving, not even slightly. It was as if they were frozen in place. I wondered why they were there or what kept them so still, but the crystal ball offered no further details, only silence.

I kept my focus on the figures, letting the shapes settle and fade, hoping something more might reveal itself with time. I felt a strange pull to keep looking, as if the scene was trying to show me something, but the harder I focused, the hazier the details became. Eventually, the figures dissolved back into the glass, leaving me with nothing but my own reflection staring back.

I want to try again tomorrow, in the daytime, of course. Maybe, with more practice, the images will become clearer, the way my connection with the Lost Souls has slowly become clearer.

CLOSER BUT STILL UNKNOWN AS SHADOWED FIGURES EMERGE

October 29, 2024

Today, I returned to the crystal ball, hoping for another glimpse of the shadowed figures I'd seen a few days ago. There's something about that dark, enclosed space, its vague familiarity and its stillness. I wanted to see if I could bring the scene into sharper focus, even slightly, and understand it better.

It didn't take long for the shapes to appear again. This time, the figures were clearer, though still obscured by the same murky haze. I could make out the barest hint of facial features: eyes glinting faintly, shadows suggesting the contours of noses, and outlines of mouths that stayed closed and still. It was enough to tell they had expressions, though whatever they were feeling was still hard to read.

As I watched, I noticed something else: slight, almost imperceptible movements. An arm shifted here, a leg adjusted there, but the movements were slow, barely noticeable, like they were happening in slow motion. It was as though they were caught in the middle of a thought, right on the edge of moving freely, but held back by something.

I kept my focus on them, hoping more details might emerge. I wonder if they know I'm watching, if those delicate movements mean they're starting to respond, or if I just missed them the first time.

Who are they? Now I have something else to figure out. Maybe next time, with enough patience, I'll see more.

CANDLE FACE VICTIM #44: THE LOST SOUL FROM BRYAN, TEXAS

November 2, 2024

I had been practicing with the crystal ball again, trying to refine my focus. Usually, it's just shadows or flickers of movement, nothing clear or tangible, except for those two times Candle Face's image appeared. But tonight was different. Tonight, the glass seemed almost alive, swirling with an energy I hadn't felt before.

As I peered deeper into the mist, something began to take shape. At first, it was just a faint outline, like a smudge on the surface. But slowly, it sharpened into the unmistakable image of a young girl's face. I blinked, thinking my eyes were playing tricks on me, but the vision only grew clearer. She looked right at me, her brown eyes wide and filled with desperation.

The connection was so vivid and real that I lost myself in it for a moment. I could see her lips move, forming words I couldn't hear. Instinctively, I pulled back from the crystal ball. But as I turned, she was no longer in the glass. She was standing in the corner of the dining room as if she had stepped right out of the vision.

She was around 15 or 16 years old, Hispanic, and on the shorter side, about 5'3" with a small frame. Her clothes were torn and dirty, her face streaked with tears. Her neck was severely red and bruised. There was something vulnerable about her.

I spoke softly, not wanting to startle her. "You came through the crystal ball?" She nodded slowly, her eyes never leaving mine. I could tell she was still gathering the courage to speak, so I waited.

"How can I help you?" I asked.

She took a shaky breath and began to tell me her story:

"I was from Bryan, Texas," she said. "It all started when I got mixed up with some friends who told me about her." She glanced nervously at the crystal ball on my desk, as though it might bring Candle Face back to listen.

"They didn't call her Candle Face," she continued, shaking her head. "To them, she was just a girl ghost, someone who died in a fire and came back to help those who needed it. My friends said she only asked for one thing in return: faith. If you believed in her, really believed, she'd solve your problems. At least, that's what they told me."

Her hands trembled, and she clasped them together.

"At first, I thought it was just a joke, a way to pass the time. But some of my friends started seeing things, feeling her presence. One of them swore that she appeared in her room one night, promising to protect her from bad things."

Her voice cracked on the last words, and she looked down, her eyes filling with tears. I waited.

"They invited me to one of their meetings," she said. "I didn't think much of it, just a bunch of us in a friend's garage, lighting candles, talking about how she could help us if we had faith. But soon, it got serious. They started saying we had to prove our loyalty to her, that she needed our devotion. I tried to back out, but by then, it was too late."

She paused as if reliving the moment.

"One night, they took me to this old, abandoned house outside town. They said it was a test of faith. I thought it was just another game, but when I got there, there were four men I'd never seen before. They were older, rough, and they had this look in their eyes."

Her voice became hoarse, barely audible.

"They said I needed to prove I truly believed in her. That's when they grabbed me. The first man forced me down and climbed on top of me, pressing his hands around my neck, just for ten seconds. Then another took his turn. They kept going, making a game out of it. Ten seconds each, then longer. Twenty seconds. Thirty. Each time they let go, they laughed, like it was some kind of sick joke. I could barely breathe, and everything was starting to fade."

She brought her hands to her throat, as if feeling their grip all over again.

"I thought it was over, that I was fixin' to die. But something in me refused to give up. I tried to fight back. I clawed at the man on top of me, trying to pull his hands away. That's when he saw it, the tiny cross tattoo on my right hand."

Her eyes widened, her voice quickening.

"His face changed. It was like he'd seen a ghost. He let go of my neck and stumbled back, like he was struck by something. 'Oh no, not a cross,' he said, his voice shaking. And just like that, all four of them dropped to the ground, gasping for air."

I leaned in closer, captivated by her story. "What happened next?" I asked.

She drew in a shaky breath. "I stood up, still gasping for air, and held out my hand toward them. I don't know where the words came from, but I shouted, 'In the name of Jesus, I demand that you leave me alone!' They kept writhing on the ground like they were in pain. For a second, I thought it had worked."

A bitter smile crossed her lips.

"But then, they started laughing. It was this awful, hollow sound. They stood up like nothing had happened. One of them sneered at me and said, 'You really thought we were in pain? You thought your little cross would save you? Only in the movies, sweetheart.'"

"Before I could run, they were on me again. And this time, they didn't stop. They strangled me until everything went black."

I watched her carefully as she finished her story, her form flickering slightly as though she were fading.

"How can I help you?" I asked again, my voice softer now, almost pleading.

Her eyes darted around the dining room as the lights in the kitchen flickered. She stepped closer, her voice barely more than a whisper. "You, you can't help me," she said, her voice breaking. "But maybe you can help the others. I was the last..."

My heart sank. "The last of what?"

"They know you're helping us," she said, her voice cracking. "But they don't care. It's all... it's all just..."

Before she could finish, her form suddenly stiffened, her eyes widening in terror. She let out a strangled gasp, as if an invisible force had tightened around her throat. I reached out instinctively, but she flickered violently and vanished, leaving only a cold, oppressive silence in her wake.

I stood there, my hand still outstretched. Whatever she was about to reveal, it was something I wasn't meant to know.

Just as I turned to leave, I heard a faint "Hide."

The lights flickered once, and then, just as quickly, they returned to a dim, steady glow. I was left standing alone, wondering what it meant.

Personal Note to My Readers (November 4, 2024)

I've been reflecting on my encounter with the lost soul who appeared to me through the crystal ball. There's a lot I'm still trying to piece together, but her words have been haunting me ever since.

She told me, "You can't help me." I keep asking myself what she meant by that. Was she saying it because she truly believed I was powerless to change her fate? Or was she warning me that something, or someone, was making it impossible for me to help her? Or did she feel I wasn't capable of helping her, since I don't have a good record of helping the Lost Souls? I've only identified seven or so of the 42 Lost Souls who have come to me. It felt like she had accepted that whatever had happened to her was beyond saving. But why would Candle Face allow her to come to me at all if I couldn't do anything to help? Perhaps I've been allowed to see these souls only to witness their torment.

And then there's her statement, "I was the last." That line keeps replaying in my mind. Does it mean she was the final soul to be allowed through to me? Is Candle Face closing the door on these visits? If that's true, then why? Has something changed on the other side? Or was it simply a warning that from now on, any attempt to help would come with even greater risks? The more I think about it, the more it feels like this was meant to leave me questioning everything I've been trying to do.

But what haunts me most is the faint whisper I heard at the end: "Hide." Who said it? Was it the lost soul, trying to protect me in her last moments? Or could it have been something else, or someone else, reaching out through the crystal ball? And who was the warning really for? Was it directed at me, urging me to prepare for something coming my way? Or was it meant for other Lost Souls trying to reach me?

Every encounter I've had so far has left me with more questions than answers, but this one felt different. The way she vanished and the flickering lights made it seem as if something or someone was trying to cut off my connection to these Lost Souls. Maybe the whisper was a plea, or maybe it was a command. But one thing is certain: I can't ignore it.

If any of you have thoughts, ideas, or your own experiences that might shed light on this, I'd be grateful to hear them. For now, all I can do is stay vigilant, try to understand the warnings, and continue searching for answers. Because if there's one thing I've learned, it's that the truth won't reveal itself easily.

Thank you for reading, and as always, stay safe.

IDENTIFIED? - CANDLE FACE VICTIMS #40 AND #41: THE RANCHER AND HIS WIFE

November 7, 2024

A little over a month ago, I shared a journal entry about a visit from two Lost Souls, a couple who appeared in my living room one night when I couldn't sleep. The man was hesitant at first, but they eventually shared their story. They described how they once lived peacefully on a ranch east of Austin, Texas, until their lives fell apart when the woman began hearing tormenting voices from Candle Face after losing faith in her. The voices wore her down until her husband, in a desperate attempt to end her suffering, took her life with a gun. Their story grew even darker when the husband himself was shot by their son, who acted out of anger and misunderstanding, convinced that his father was abandoning him. The couple's remains were buried together, and their story was lost to time, while Candle Face kept their spirits in her Lair and continued their torment.

This couple's story didn't feel like a simple recounting of suffering. It included specific details that felt like clues. I felt compelled to dig deeper and see whether historical records supported their story.

With that in mind, I started researching. The couple had mentioned a ranch east of Austin, the man's Mexican heritage, and a death involving a firearm. To start, I used Google and tried search terms like "elderly couple disappearance Texas ranch," "missing couple gun ranch Austin," and "Texas couple killed." At first, I kept hitting dead ends and unrelated cases. Then something caught my eye. An article described an unsolved case from 1976 about an elderly couple who vanished from their ranch under circumstances very similar to what the Lost Souls had told me.

Comparing the Two Stories

The Lost Souls

During our encounter, the elderly man said he ended his wife's life to free her from the torment Candle Face had inflicted on her. He also described the steps he took to cover it up. He specifically mentioned that the bathroom door had a bullet hole in it, which he couldn't repair, so he took it off its hinges and hid it in the barn under a pile of hay. He also said he was shot by their son, who believed, in a fit of rage, that his father was abandoning him. Their son then buried their bodies together in South Texas.

The Article

The article described an unsolved case involving an elderly couple who disappeared from their rural ranch east of Austin in 1976. Investigators found signs of violence: a bullet hole in a window, bloodstains, and a missing bedroom door that was later discovered hidden in a barn on the property. Authorities considered different motives, from family conflict to outside involvement, but the couple's bodies were never found, leaving the case unsolved.

Key Similarities

1. **Location and Background:** Both the couple who visited me and the couple in the article lived on a ranch east of Austin. In both accounts, the husband had roots in Mexico.

2. **Unusual Circumstances of Death:** Both stories involve a missing door and evidence of gunshots. The man who visited me explicitly mentioned hiding a door with a bullet hole in the barn, while the article noted that investigators found a hidden door in the barn during their search.

3. **Family Conflict:** In both stories, the son played a tragic role and acted in anger.

4. **Torment by Voices:** In both accounts, the woman seemed to be pushed to her breaking point by cruel, relentless voices. Those voices may have been Candle Face's way of breaking her down and forcing her husband into a mercy killing.

Key Differences

1. **Confession vs. Theories:** The couple who visited me shared their story as a direct confession, filling in details that investigators could only speculate about. The article, on the other hand, presented theories based on limited evidence and left much of the story unclear.

2. **Direct Contact:** The Lost Souls came to me directly, seemingly to set the record straight and tell their side of the story. The article is built from small details and speculation from the authorities, without the direct account I received during the encounter.

Despite the similarities, I could still be wrong. The parallels between the Lost Souls' story and the historical case are strong, but it's possible that I'm misreading their messages or that Candle Face's manipulations have distorted the details. For that reason, I can't definitively say that the couple who visited me and the individuals in the article are one and the same.

Out of respect for any surviving family members who may still be searching for answers, I won't reveal their names here. But you can do your own research. My goal is to honor the spirits who reach out to me and share their stories in a way that respects their pain without causing more harm.

Whether these two stories are truly connected or not, these souls are still reaching out for closure. And as Candle Face continues to kill, I'll continue to listen, to give them a voice, and to push back against the evil she spreads.

CANDLE FACE CHRONICLES: THE NIGHT I BECAME THE MURDERER

November 9, 2024

The Lost Souls' testimonies are becoming more vivid with each visit, bringing clearer images and sharper details. I've been documenting every word, every glimpse of their final moments, hoping to piece together the facts behind their deaths. But even with the increased clarity, some crucial details remain out of reach. It's like trying to put together a jigsaw puzzle with missing pieces, always feeling close but never quite there.

I've tried everything: late nights, revisiting old notes, even trying new techniques. But despite my efforts, I've hit a wall. For a year now, I've reached out to the paranormal community, investigators, psychics, mediums, anyone who might lend their expertise to help with the identities of these Lost Souls and the stories behind their deaths. Every time, it's the same response. They're too busy, too wrapped up in their own pursuits. The disappointment is real. What happened to the sense of unity within the paranormal field? What happened to the willingness to help others?

Finding readers has been just as difficult. I'm competing against millions of other authors. Everyone is chasing the next viral story, the sensational headline that will get clicks, likes, and sales. Meanwhile, I'm here trying to solve real cases, trying to bring peace to these souls who haunt me every night, and it feels like no one's listening. It's relentless, this frustration. I'm practically begging for readers to get involved and share their thoughts, but it often feels like I'm screaming and no one hears me.

Every now and then, I question if all of this is worth it. The exhaustion of trying to reach a disinterested audience is wearing me down. But then, late at night, when the Lost Souls return, desperate and pleading, I know I can't turn away. I can't abandon them. I keep hoping they might offer fresh clues if I can just get a few dedicated readers to notice. It's not just wishful thinking. More eyes, more minds can sometimes catch what I miss, especially when the memories are broken.

But here I am again, finding that I'm mostly on my own. It's a lonely road, but it's the one I chose. I've said it before. I know I have to do the heavy lifting. Even so, there's always a part of me that hopes someone, somewhere, will step forward to help.

Tonight, I decided to stop waiting for help. I decided to push my abilities as far as I could. Instead of waiting for another lost soul to appear with a half-ass testimony, I took matters into my own hands. The idea came to me in a moment of frustration: what if I could see through the eyes of the killers? What if I could use remote viewing and the crystal ball to become the one who took their lives?

I dimmed the lights in my dining room. I could feel the tension in the air, as if the very shadows were watching, waiting to see what I would do. I placed my hands on the crystal ball, the cold surface familiar yet different this time, almost as if it were resisting me. My fingers trembled slightly.

The mist inside the ball began to swirl, faster and faster, as if something within it was waking up. I could feel it pulling at me, a strange, almost magnetic force. For a moment, I hesitated. Was this really the path I wanted to take? Was I prepared for what I might see? But it was too late to turn back. I closed my eyes, letting go of everything: my identity, my thoughts, my fears. I let the crystal ball pull me in.

And then, suddenly, everything shifted. I was no longer myself. I was him: the killer.

The Vision (The Killer's Point of View)

I pace the room and try not to hit her. The whiskey sits hot in my gut, and every word out of her mouth makes it worse. Bills. Drinking. The way I act around people. Same old crap. She keeps at it like I'm supposed to stand there and take it.

"Why can't you just be quiet for once?" I yell.

She keeps talking.

My jaw aches from clenching it. My hands will not stay still. My knuckles are still split from the last time I punched the wall. She sees how mad I am and keeps going anyway, looking at me like I'm nothing.

I try to hold it in. I tell myself to walk out, sit down, do anything else. But she will not stop. She always has to keep going. Always one more word. Always one more look.

Then she spits at me.

It hits my cheek and the corner of my mouth. Warm. Wet. For a second, everything goes blank. Then I hit her. Hard. My fist lands before I even know I moved. Her face jerks to the side and she drops.

I go down with her, close enough to smell blood and sweat. Her eyes are still open. Still looking at me like she isn't scared. Like she's still better than me.

"I'm sorry," I say, but I don't mean it. I just want her quiet.

Then she spits at me again.

That tears the last bit of control out of me.

"You don't get to look at me like that!"

I get to my feet and bring my boot down on her head. I feel it all the way up my leg. I do it again. And again. Blood jumps across the floor and walls. Bone gives under my heel. I keep stomping until her face is gone and the room is finally quiet.

I stand there trying to breathe. My chest burns. My hands will not stop shaking. I look down at her and lean toward what is left of her right ear.

"Carmen, you should've just listened."

Then the panic hits.

She wasn't supposed to die tonight.

I stare at what is left of her and feel the liquor clear just enough for the fear to get in.

"She's going to be furious," I say to the empty room. "I was supposed to wait. I was supposed to sacrifice you later."

What have I done?

Personal Note to My Readers

After that vision, I couldn't get past the name I heard him say: Carmen. The experience was so vivid, so visceral, that even after coming back to myself, I could still feel his rage, the force of each brutal strike of his boot, and the twisted satisfaction that came with it. I went back through my old journal entries, combing through them for anything that might connect. And then it hit me. On June 5, 2024, a spirit had come to me, identifying herself as Cayman. She spoke of a violent death at the hands of her husband, but at the time, I wasn't certain if that was her real name or if I had simply misunderstood. What convinces me now is one specific overlap between that earlier testimony and tonight's vision: in both accounts, she spat at him twice. That's too exact to dismiss.

After living through this vision tonight, I'm starting to believe that I wasn't just witnessing a killer's memories. I was the killer.

The realization is almost too much to bear. I believe I became the husband, the one who killed Candle Face Victim #32, whom I had documented as Clean Shaven. Everything lines up: the rage, the twisted justifications, the spitting, the panic when he realized he had killed her too soon, and the name Carmen spoken in that final moment.

Writing about this experience was more difficult than anything I've done before. For the first time, the testimony pulled me into the moment until I felt trapped inside it. I became the killer, feeling his anger, his intoxicated thrill, his need to silence her. I was inside his reality, carrying out his violent actions as if they were my own. Remote viewing and the crystal ball didn't just show me his memories. They pulled me into his mind. I could see, feel, and think everything he did. In a strange twist, I've become interactive with the Lost Souls' killers instead of my readers being interactive with me.

This new ability is something I never expected. It's powerful and terrifying. For a year now, I've documented the Lost Souls' accounts from a certain distance. Now, I've crossed a line I never imagined I would. I'm no longer just listening to their stories. I'm becoming part of them, stepping into the very people who ended their lives.

It's hard to describe the fear that comes with this realization. If I can slip into the mind of a killer this easily, what does that mean for me? Am I losing myself in the process? Will I be able to control it? Remote viewing and the crystal ball have unlocked something in me, something I'm not sure I can control or even want to. The question that haunts me now is this: how far will this ability take me? Will it help solve these cases, or will it consume me entirely?

For now, I have to keep piecing together the lives of these Lost Souls, hoping to find answers and closure. I'm left wondering who I'm becoming, and whether there will come a time when I can no longer tell the difference between myself and the memories I'm inhabiting.

I can't stop now. I owe it to these Lost Souls to keep going, no matter the cost. Every time I reach for that crystal ball, I wonder if this might be the moment I lose myself for good.

CANDLE FACE CHRONICLES: THE RHYTHMIC CONNECTION

November 12, 2024

Everyone was asleep, and I was ready to practice my remote viewing and mediumship skills. I sat at the dining room table, preparing to call on a lost soul. I had the crystal ball in front of me. After a long, stressful day, I just wanted to focus on something familiar, something I could control. But a lost soul had other plans for me.

As I was getting ready, the kitchen lights began flickering. I know what this means. A nocturnal visitor was on the way. But tonight, something was different.

No one appeared, but the flickering followed a rhythm, almost like it had a pulse of its own. I stayed at the table, watching as the lights flashed in quick, deliberate bursts, then paused, only to start again. It felt like the house itself was trying to get my attention.

Then, without warning, a strange, crushing pressure gripped my chest. My heart started to race, beating so hard it felt like it would burst. The pain was sudden, a searing line of fire across my left side. I clutched at my chest, my mind racing. Was this it? Was I having a heart attack?

My breaths came in short, shallow gasps. The room began to darken, my vision blurring. I could feel the blood rushing in my ears, drowning out every other sound. The pressure in my chest only grew worse, like a vice tightening around my ribs, squeezing the life out of me.

That's when I noticed it. My heartbeat matched the flickering lights in the kitchen. Flash. Thud. Flash. Thud.

The pounding continued, relentless, and as I focused, it started to sound like a drumbeat. The rhythm was deep, raw, almost primal, like someone striking a drum with bare hands. Each beat seemed to echo through my chest. It had a wooden, hollow resonance to it, almost like someone striking a hand drum. The sound was distinct, unlike anything I had heard before.

And then everything shifted.

I was no longer sitting at my dining room table. I was in the woods. The scent of wet leaves and damp earth filled my nostrils. The humid air stung my lungs with every forced breath. I was running. My legs felt heavy, my breath shallow and panicked. The drumbeat was relentless, pounding in my chest and ears, driving me forward along a path deeper into the woods.

I couldn't see where I was going, only that I had to keep moving. The trees seemed to shift and dance around me. My heart continued to pound in my chest, the rhythm urging me on, faster and faster. I followed the path to a clearing. That's where I saw them: three shadowy figures. They stood like sentinels, their eyes and chests glowing faintly. The familiar drumbeat grew louder, more frantic.

"You have failed her," they chanted in unison.

Suddenly, she appeared, Candle Face, her face a twisted, melted mask illuminated by a backdrop of flames. The heat of her presence was overwhelming, and I could feel it searing into my skin. The drumbeat became deafening.

"You sought perfection in your music yet ignored my demands, Jacob," Candle Face said. "You were to bring me those who did not believe, yet you chose not to obey. Now, you will pay the price."

The shadows closed in, and everything went black.

And just like that, I was back at my dining room table. The lights had stopped flickering, the drumbeat had faded, leaving only the pain in my chest. My hands were shaking, my heart still pounding as if it were trying to catch up with reality.

Personal Note to My Readers (November 13, 2024)

During the vision, Candle Face referred to me as Jacob. At first, I was confused. Clearly, Candle Face knows who I am, so why did she call me Jacob? Was it some kind of psychological trick? For a while, I was convinced that I had become the target, that she was trying to toy with me.

As I reflected on the experience, trying to make sense of what I had just witnessed, pieces of it started to fall into place. The drumbeat, the shadows, the overwhelming sense of dread. It all felt too familiar.

That's when it hit me: this wasn't the first time I had connected with this lost soul. On March 22, 2024, he came to me, desperate to share his story about shadows pursuing him in the woods. Back then, I only heard his words, but tonight, I lived through his eyes. I witnessed what he experienced on the day he died. For a few terrifying minutes, I became the lost soul, Candle Face Victim #21.

What troubles me most is that I didn't consciously use the crystal ball or any of my remote viewing techniques. The moment my heartbeat synced with the flickering lights, it was as if the crystal ball activated on its own. I was pulled into a vision, and I wasn't in control. It felt like the lost soul was reaching out to me, forcing the connection.

The rhythm of the drumbeat felt like a message, a cry for help. I can't help but think that this experience was a warning, both for me and for all of us trying to piece together these memories. I've always relied on my remote viewing techniques with some degree of control, but tonight shattered that sense of safety.

If anyone reading this has experienced something similar, if you've felt your abilities start to activate without your intent, I need your help. The Lost Souls are counting on us to understand what they're trying to communicate, but I fear I'm opening doors that I won't be able to close. There's something hidden in that drumbeat, something urgent that I need to understand. I can't do it alone.

Please reach out if you have any ideas. The Lost Souls, perhaps even my sanity and safety, depend on what we discover together.

CANDLE FACE CHRONICLES: SEARCHING FOR THE MAN BEHIND THE DRUMBEAT

November 14, 2024

Two nights ago, I experienced something truly troubling. Even now, as I sit at my desk, the drumbeat is still in my mind. It follows me wherever I go, as if it's trying to tell me something I still can't understand. Or maybe Candle Face planted the sound in my head to drive me insane, the way she does with so many of her victims.

I now know that the lost soul's name is Jacob. But who was he, really? The name alone doesn't tell me much. I'm convinced he was the creator of that drumbeat, the one that resonated through my chest and synced with the kitchen lights. But I need to know more. Who was he? What led him to that encounter with Candle Face and her shadows?

When I compare the two encounters, one from March 22, 2024, and the other from November 12, 2024, I can see the case more clearly. The first time Jacob came to me, back in March, he was desperate, speaking of shadows pursuing him relentlessly. It was terrifying, but back then, I could only hear his words. I knew nothing about remote viewing at the time. I felt his fear. There was still some distance between us.

This time, the connection was deeper and more immediate. His testimony pulled me into his experience. I felt what he felt and saw what he saw. When Candle Face referred to me as "Jacob," I was confused at first. I thought she had mistaken me for him, or maybe she was trying to manipulate me. But as the vision continued, it became clear: For that moment, his identity swallowed mine. I had become Jacob.

I was witnessing Jacob's final moments, the day he was taken by Candle Face and her shadows. The vision revealed flashes of his terror, and the frantic drumbeat that was both something he created with his own hands and a signal of his death. But why did Candle Face target him? What was it about Jacob that drew her to him? According to his March testimony, she killed him because he didn't follow her orders. But what were those orders? In other cases, the Lost Souls have said they were supposed to kill nonbelievers but refused. Was that Jacob's role too? Did his refusal get him killed?

As I try to piece together more details, I've gone back through my journal entries and the scattered clues he left behind. Jacob spoke of shadows in the woods, of a perfect rhythm that called to him, a sound he could never quite replicate. That obsession pulled him into the forest, where he met his end.

Now, I feel an urgent need to know more. Was he from Central Texas, like so many of the other Lost Souls who have reached out to me? Was he a local musician whose drumbeat was a signature sound that somehow led him to Candle Face? Learning Jacob's identity matters to Jacob, to my own understanding, and to the other Lost Souls who continue to reach out, desperate for help.

I'm turning to the internet, hoping to figure out who Jacob was and where he came from. If you, my readers, have any information or can help me piece together Jacob's story, please reach out. Together, we can solve this case, find out where he lived, and perhaps discover what led him into the woods.

In the meantime, I'll keep listening to that drumbeat. Not that I have much of a choice. Maybe it'll reveal the answers we need.

CANDLE FACE, JACOB, AND THE UNFINISHED BEAT

November 17, 2024

Now I know the name of the lost soul who reached out to me in March and whose final moments I relived just a few nights ago. His name is Jacob, but that discovery only brought more questions. Determined to find out who he was, I turned to the internet and searched for every clue I could find. I began with the testimony he gave me back in March and the name "Jacob" that Candle Face revealed during the vision a few days ago.

I started by Googling his name paired with "Missing Central Texas," but nothing useful came up. So I refined the search, swapping "Central Texas" with specific towns and cities: Austin, Round Rock, and Georgetown. Still nothing. It wasn't until I tried "San Marcos" that something clicked. Suddenly, multiple hits appeared about a man named Jacob Newhouse from San Marcos, a college town south of Austin.

Jacob Newhouse, according to several local news reports, was 45 years old when he disappeared last year. He was last seen on November 28, 2023, and was found dead on December 9, 2023. The reports say foul play wasn't suspected, though they did mention concerns about his mental health. Some sources suggested he might have been suicidal.

Read the news report here: https://www.fox7austin.com/news/missing-san-marcos-texas-jacob-newhouse

After finding his name, I turned to Facebook, hoping to learn more about this man who may have visited me as a lost soul. I found an account belonging to a Jacob Newhouse from San Marcos. The most recent posts were emotional, two desperate pleas for help on November 29, 2023, asking if anyone had seen him. These posts were made after Jacob went missing. According to a comment thread, someone had found Jacob's phone and used it to send out those distress posts.

Scrolling through his older posts, I came across one from October 23, 2023. It showed a dirt path sloping down into a dense wooded area. The scene was similar to the one I saw in my vision. Could this be the exact place where Jacob ran, fleeing from shadows?

I stumbled upon a video post from October 5, 2023. In the video, Jacob was playing on what looked like a leather-bound instrument, maybe a makeshift drum or even a suitcase. As I hit play, my heart skipped a beat. The rhythm was the exact drumbeat I heard during my vision. The same beat that synchronized with my heartbeat and the flickering lights in my kitchen. The caption under the video simply read: "Help me… sound is… incomplete!!!"

Facebook: https://www.facebook.com/reel/309976765008005

I played the video over and over, trying to make sense of it. The beat was relentless, almost hypnotic, and Jacob seemed proud of it and frustrated by it at the same time. At the end of the clip, he abruptly stopped, shaking his head and waving his arms in frustration. That's when I realized what he meant by "…incomplete." Jacob was searching for the perfect ending, an elusive conclusion to his music. And in both his March testimony and my vision, Candle Face taunted him, mocking his obsessive search for musical perfection.

The connection is too strong to ignore. Candle Face called me Jacob in the vision, and I found a "Jacob" who lived in San Marcos, played the same drumbeat, and went missing shortly before being found dead. What are the odds?

Personal Note to My Readers

I know some of you may notice something different in this journal entry. I included his name this time, even though I previously said I wouldn't reveal the names of the Lost Souls out of respect for their living relatives. The truth is, I'm struggling with this decision every single day. How can I truly help these Lost Souls if I can't reveal who I think they are? After all, the souls come to me to be identified. They want their stories told, their names spoken. If I don't name them, what good is the information I discover? Intelligence, after all, must be actionable.

But is this the right action? By revealing names, am I helping them find peace, or am I dragging their families into a nightmare they never asked for? Am I opening wounds that should stay closed? What if I got the identities wrong?

I don't know what to do. I feel like I'm walking a razor's edge between helping these souls and violating the privacy of their loved ones. If I reach out to Jacob's family, will they see it as an act of compassion, or will they call me a freak, another lunatic obsessed with ghosts? I fear the latter, yet the pull to do something is almost unbearable.

I'm asking you, my readers, for your guidance. Should I continue to name these Lost Souls, even if it risks causing pain to their families? Should I reach out directly to their loved ones, knowing I might be branded as some sort of monster? Or do I keep their names hidden, knowing that this might mean leaving their stories unfinished, their souls still bound to Candle Face?

I don't have the answers. I'm just trying to find a way to do right by these souls who reach out to me, and by their families who may or may not want to know what happened. If you have any advice, please let me know.

I'm haunted by Jacob's drumbeat, by the plea in his music. Is it a cry for help, a message he's desperate for me to understand? Or is it simply the beat of a lost soul who can't find his way home?

The Lost Souls are counting on us, and so am I.

While the name "Jacob" was revealed to me in a vision, I want to clarify that any connection to real individuals, including Jacob Newhouse from San Marcos, is based on publicly available information and shouldn't be taken as definitive proof. My intention isn't to cause distress to any living relatives. I'm trying to understand and help those who reach out to me.

CANDLE FACE VICTIM #45: THE FRIEND WHO DIDN'T ANSWER

November 21, 2024

I was sitting in the living room watching TV when the kitchen lights began to flicker. By now, I know what that means. The sunroom door creaked open, and a young Hispanic woman in her early twenties walked in. Her expression was somber, her eyes hollow, and a wide, jagged hole had been torn through her translucent forehead. Violence had marked her death. There was no doubt about that.

"My name is Lupe," she began, quiet but firm. "I need you to hear what happened to me. I need someone to know the truth."

I gestured for her to sit, but she stayed standing and went straight into her story.

"I was 21 when they killed me," she said. "That night, in 1993, I left my little girl with my parents to visit a friend. I parked in front of her house, but she didn't answer when I knocked. She was expecting me, so I didn't understand why she wasn't home. Confused and upset, I decided to leave."

Her voice grew louder, anger twisting her expression as she turned away from me. "I never made it to my car."

She turned back to face me. "Some men were standing outside my friend's house. I didn't know them, but I smiled as I passed. That's when I saw it. A dark truck creeping down the street."

She clenched her hands, her translucent fingers trembling slightly. "I didn't even have time to react. The window rolled down, and I saw the barrel of a rifle pointing out. There was a loud crack. One of the guys by the curb grabbed his leg and fell, screaming. And then..."

She paused, reaching up to touch the hole in her head. "And then the second shot came. It hit me here." Her voice softened. "I didn't even feel it at first. I just collapsed. I could still see them, the men in the truck. One of them smiled at me. He was wearing a hat. And then they drove off, like it was nothing."

Her voice faltered, and for a moment, she was silent. I waited, then asked gently, "Were you the target? It sounds like the men were the targets."

"No," she replied firmly, bitterness in her tone. "I was the target. Those men, they killed me for her."

"Who?" I asked, though the answer was already forming in my mind.

"Really, you have to ask?" Her voice sharpened. "You know who I mean. She's the one they worship, the one they kill for. I didn't know it then. I saw her later. After I died."

Lupe's form flickered as she continued, her words coming faster now, as though she feared time was slipping away. "I woke up in a place I can barely describe," she said, her voice trembling. "It was dark in a way that didn't feel like night. The shadows themselves were alive. There were others there, trapped, silent, their faces blurred like smudged glass. I screamed, but no sound came out. That's when I saw her."

"She stood in front of me, her face burned, melted, twisted into something no one should ever have to see. She didn't speak. I felt her watching me, studying me. And then she smiled, like she was pleased. Pleased that I was there."

But something didn't sit right. "Why you?" I asked. "Why were you targeted?"

Lupe hesitated, looking toward the floor. "It was random." Her voice wavered.

"Was it really random? Or was there more to it?"

Her eyes welled with tears, and she finally looked back at me. "There was a time I laughed at my friend. She believed in this ghost, a ghost that helps people but kills those who don't believe. I thought it was ridiculous. I told her so. She got angry, but I didn't think it mattered."

"Do you think your friend had something to do with this? Did she know you'd be attacked? Is that why she asked you to come over and didn't answer the door?"

Lupe's form shook, her tears falling silently. "Maybe. Maybe that's why she called me over but didn't answer the door. Maybe she knew."

Her voice broke, and she began to sob. "She was my friend. I trusted her."

She wiped at her face, though the tears left no trace. "I didn't understand then, but I do now. Candle Face's followers, they're everywhere. They watch, they listen, and they choose. My death was a warning. A punishment. I laughed at the wrong story, and for that, they killed me."

The lights stopped flickering, and the room went still and quiet. Lupe turned and walked slowly back to the shadow without another word.

Personal Note to My Readers

Lupe said Candle Face's followers are everywhere. What does that mean? Are they confined to Central Texas, where most of the victims are, or do they stretch beyond to other parts of the state, the country, or even the world?

Then there's the question of truth. Was Lupe truly killed for Candle Face, or was her death just another act of violence? She wanted me to know the truth, so why did she say it was random? Was she protecting her friend, even though she may have been involved in her death?

Truth and belief are tangled together here. Belief in Candle Face, in justice, in hope, all of it shapes how we see what happened.

So I have to ask: What do you believe?

CANDLE FACE CHRONICLES: THE MASTER SHADOW COMETH

December 2, 2024

Tonight, I tried something I've done before with success. Sitting before the crystal ball, I focused harder than ever, pushing myself to connect with a lost soul. I wanted to slip into their world, to see what they saw at the moment they were killed by Candle Face or her followers. Maybe I could find better clues about who they were and who killed them.

The kitchen lights flickered, faint at first and then violently, snapping me out of my trance. I turned, and there she was, a young woman in her mid-twenties, with an oddly warm presence despite her ghostly form. Her face bore a sad but gentle expression, her voice soft as she greeted me with a simple, "Hello."

Honestly, I was hoping to avoid a nocturnal visitor tonight, just me and the crystal ball. Low-key séance vibes. But there she was, standing in my dining room like she owned the place.

As she began to speak, the crystal ball between us changed. The soft light inside turned dark, swirling violently. Intense heat settled over me, and she stopped speaking mid-sentence, her eyes darting toward the ball. Her form flickered, unstable, as she turned to me and then toward the ceiling.

"Hide!" she screamed, her voice breaking. Her ghostly outline shimmered, and for a moment, it felt like the room was about to collapse under her panic.

It happened quickly. A shadow poured from the crystal ball, expanding and solidifying into a humanoid form with the same evil presence I'd only felt when Candle Face visited me. Its edges flickered like smoke. It spoke in a low, throaty voice, each word vibrating through my chest.

"I am the shadow of Candle Face," it said, its form towering over me. "For months, something has been amiss here. Energy out of place. I've come to see why."

I sat frozen, unable to speak. The lost soul who had been with me moments before was gone, vanished as if she had never been there.

The shadow's massive hand clamped around my neck, lifting me off the ground. Its touch was scorching, so hot it felt like its hand and my neck fused together. My feet dangled uselessly as I gasped for air, my vision darkening at the edges.

It carried me through the house, its presence sucking the cool early December air from the rooms. It visited every corner, even stopping in my bedroom, where my wife slept peacefully, oblivious to the nightmare I was going through.

When we reached the upstairs bedroom, the shadow paused, tilting its head as if listening, sniffing the air. My heart thundered in my chest, each beat begging it to move on. After a long moment, it did.

Back downstairs, it threw me to the ground with a force that left me gasping.

"You think you're clever," it said, stepping closer. Its eyes, or what passed for them, flicked downward, focusing on the crystal ball. "But shadows see everything."

Its gaze remained on the crystal ball, a red glow swirling faintly in the glass. It felt like the crystal ball itself was alive, its surface somehow part of my pain.

I managed to blurt out, "Who are you?"

Then, almost like it was playing with me, it leaned closer and whispered a riddle:

> *I was freed to kill but bound again.*
> *My name is yelled, though I bring silence.*
> *Look where the broom sweeps, and you'll find my mark.*

The shadow began to dissipate, retreating back into the crystal ball. Before it disappeared completely, it turned to me one last time.

"I'll be back," it said. "And next time, I won't just be looking."

The room was silent again. I sat there, staring at the crystal ball. Freed to kill, bound again. The broom. The mark.

I didn't need to solve it to know one thing: something terrible had been set into motion.

PARANORMAL PODCASTS: TOO BUSY, TOO SCARED

December 8, 2024

For two months, I've been searching for a paranormal podcaster willing to host a meeting between Mr. Smoe and me. The goal was to discuss the conflicting views on Candle Face. According to Mr. Smoe, who says he's a Candle Face Disciple, she's a compassionate spirit who helps those in need. That view doesn't match her ruthless killings of non-believers. I thought a discussion like that would interest the paranormal podcast community. Instead, I've been met with excuses, fear, and disinterest.

Many say they're "too busy," while others outright refuse, admitting that Candle Face's story is too terrifying for them to touch. It's hard to square that with the image they project online: brave investigators chasing entities, taunting spirits, and claiming to face the paranormal head-on.

During one recent podcast, a popular host, someone known for his so-called bravery, admitted he was uncomfortable discussing a demon. The topic then shifted to something far less supernatural: poop. Yes, a man who claims to confront spirits was too scared to discuss a demon and chose instead to focus on excrement. If that doesn't sum up the state of paranormal entertainment, I don't know what does.

I've spoken before about my frustrations with the paranormal community. Time and again, I've had to do most of the work myself because the people I approached were either too scared or too focused on entertainment to take this seriously. Their bravery often feels like a performance that falls apart the moment real danger appears.

Still, I can't give up. The Lost Souls who visit me deserve better, and I'll continue to seek out serious members of the paranormal community who are willing to help. My hope of finding them is fading, but I owe it to the souls who depend on me to keep trying.

In the meantime, I've turned to you, my readers. You've been my most reliable allies so far, and I'm grateful for that.

FREED AND BOUND AGAIN: THE BROOMSTICK KILLER

December 15, 2024

It's been two weeks since Candle Face's Master Shadow left me a riddle to figure out who he is. My mind has been on overdrive since then, trying to put it all together. I've been sitting at my desk for hours now, hunched over my computer and a stack of notes, with a stiff neck and burning eyes. It's well past 3:00 a.m., and I can still feel the lingering heat in the air from that night two weeks ago. My wife is asleep down the hall, blissfully unaware of the chaos I've allowed into our home. The crystal ball rests on the center of my bookshelf behind me like a guilty secret. It's been inert in the days since the attack, its surface clear and still. No sparks of red light flicker inside. No silhouettes swirl within. Yet I know what happened was real. My throat is still a bit sore from where that monstrous hand hoisted me into the air.

Before I lose my mind, I need to document the results of my investigation. Two weeks ago, after the Master Shadow vanished back into the crystal ball, it left me with a cryptic riddle:

I was freed to kill but bound again.
My name is yelled, though I bring silence.
Look where the broom sweeps, and you'll find my mark.

Shortly after the Master Shadow's visit, I grabbed onto the first symbolic interpretation that came to mind: fire. I reasoned that fire, when unleashed, kills indiscriminately, only to be snuffed out, or "bound again," once it's contained. People shout "Fire!" in fear, yet fire's aftermath often leaves a silent, charred landscape. And ash, what remains of a burned home, must be swept up. "Look where the broom sweeps" could mean ashes. It wasn't a bad guess in my rattled state. At the time, it made sense.

But as I continued my research over these last two weeks, I realized it was too simple. The Master Shadow felt too cunning and too personal to be something as impersonal as a mere element. Its words and actions suggested a deliberate taunt, a clue meant to be solved. And so, over many late nights since the attack, I've been looking at every angle.

As a former investigator, I know that sometimes you have to list out every possibility before you can narrow them down. The riddle gave me three main clues:

1. **Freed to kill but bound again:** This suggests a cycle, someone once restrained, then released, allowed to do harm, and then restrained once more. "Bound again" strongly suggests a person who was captured, imprisoned, or otherwise contained, freed at some point, and then captured again.

2. **My name is yelled, though I bring silence:** The name is shouted, perhaps as a warning or a cry of alarm. If it's a person, their name might have been notorious, spoken in fear or anger. Yet this entity "brings silence," which might mean death. Although I first considered the word "Fire!" here, over these last two weeks I've leaned toward something more human, something that leaves lasting scars after the ashes cool.

3. **Look where the broom sweeps, and you'll find my mark:** The broom is the strangest part. Why a broom? What mark would it leave or reveal? If not ashes, could it refer to something else involving a broomstick? Or is it symbolic? Two weeks of searching helped me realize this might be literal, pointing to a killer known for using a broomstick.

Many murderers have nicknames that bring certain images to mind: Jack the Ripper, the Night Stalker, the Boston Strangler. Two weeks of late-night research and rechecking old case files still gave me nothing definitive until I searched specifically for a "Broomstick killer." That search led me to Kenneth McDuff, known as the "Broomstick Killer." Before settling on McDuff, I also considered other possibilities:

- **Mythological or Urban Legends:** I thought of witches, Baba Yaga, and the idea of "Witch!"

being yelled in old towns as a warning. But witches and broomsticks felt too mythic for a modern case. And the Master Shadow seemed tied to a more recent evil.

- **Firearms and Shouting "Fire!":** In the days after the attack, I reconsidered my first guess. Guns don't really connect with brooms, and they aren't "freed and bound" in a legal sense. That path went nowhere.

- **Other Killers or Criminals with Cyclical Freedom:** I spent many hours over the last two weeks revisiting notorious criminals who were imprisoned, released, and then went on to kill again. The U.S. criminal justice system has seen its share of such cases. Names like Ted Bundy came to mind. He escaped and killed again. But "Bundy" wasn't yelled as a warning, nor was there any broom connection. Most of those criminals lacked that unique broomstick element I needed.

Going back to the broom clue was my breakthrough. Kenneth McDuff was infamous in Texas, known for a brutal killing spree and for using a broomstick as a weapon in one of his earliest murders. He was sentenced to death, bound, then later paroled, freed, due to legal changes and prison overcrowding. He killed again and was eventually captured, tried, and executed, bound again for good. His life and crimes match the riddle almost too perfectly.

Now, does McDuff's case fit the rest of the riddle?

"My name is yelled, though I bring silence."

In Texas, McDuff's name was tied to judicial failure and terror. Communities cursed his name and shouted it in anger, protest, and outrage at the system that let him go free. In that sense, his name was yelled as a warning and condemnation. The silence he brought was the silence of the grave, his victims and their families left in mute horror.

"Look where the broom sweeps, and you'll find my mark."

McDuff earned the nickname "Broomstick Killer" because of his use of a broomstick in a murder. This line directly points to that nickname, guiding me to him as if the Master Shadow wanted me to know who he was.

Over the past two weeks, I've also connected another dot: a newspaper snippet about a prostitute named Crystal, murdered in North Austin. I recall a lost soul named Crystal who reached out to me on May 24, 2024. She mentioned her killing in North Austin. At the time, I assumed it was a Candle Face follower directly behind her murder. But now, seeing Crystal's name linked to McDuff's known or suspected victims, I'm convinced that the spirit I spoke to was one of his victims. Was McDuff a Candle Face Deliverer, killing for Candle Face, and now rewarded for his work by becoming the Master Shadow?

Had Crystal's spirit been trying to guide me toward McDuff's identity all along? Two weeks of rereading old notes and comparing dates and details suggest she may have. If Candle Face can summon or control the evil spirits of history's worst murderers, then the Master Shadow's appearance and riddle serve as an ugly test. Solving it brings equal parts satisfaction and dread.

Could there be another killer who fits this pattern? Someone else freed, bound again, associated with a broom? After extensive searching, I found no one else so clearly tied to this particular weapon. McDuff was paroled, killed again, and then executed. It's a well-documented chain of events. The broomstick detail is too specific to be a coincidence.

I should also explain why I first thought of fire. That night, two weeks ago, I was reeling from the attack. The Master Shadow's grip was searing hot, and my mind latched onto the idea of shouting "Fire!" as a warning call. In hindsight, the personal nature of the riddle, the historical weight behind it, and my investigative instincts all point to a human monster behind the fire. Fire doesn't care who it kills, and it doesn't make threats about returning. The Master Shadow does.

The fact that Candle Face can conjure or channel the spirit of a murderer like McDuff speaks to her power. McDuff's name is tied to legal failure, cruelty, and terror. That's exactly the kind of energy Candle Face might exploit.

Two weeks have passed since the Master Shadow's attack. In that time, I've grown more certain of his identity and purpose. If he truly is Kenneth McDuff's spirit, then I'm dealing with something beyond a mere haunting. Candle Face may be using the psychic remnants of killers to enforce her will or terrify those who oppose her. I think I remember from somewhere that the worst of Candle Face's followers who kill for her become shadows, but I can't remember where that came from. In any case, the Master Shadow said he'd be back. I believe him.

For now, I'll keep documenting everything. I understand more now than I did on the night of the attack. Knowledge is the only weapon I have, and I've spent the past two weeks using it to solve this riddle. The connection to Crystal's murder gives me a heartbreaking link: a victim's lost soul reached out to me months ago, and only now do I understand why that's relevant.

Naming him may be the first step toward stopping him. If I'm right about the Master Shadow's identity, then perhaps I can find a way to destroy him along with Candle Face.

I'll continue researching Candle Face's methods. How are these killers' spirits summoned or contained? Are there historical precedents for this kind of necromantic practice? Over the next days and weeks, I'll dig deeper into archives, old ritual texts, and reported hauntings. Crystal's story might hold more clues.

For tonight, I'll put these notes away. The clock is edging toward dawn, and I'm exhausted. Two weeks have passed since the nightmare began, and I've made progress. I think I've identified the figure behind the riddle. He's likely Kenneth McDuff, the Broomstick Killer. And I know he's under Candle Face's control.

The Master Shadow promised to return, but this time, I'm better prepared. I understand the enemy I face. That will have to be enough for now.

A NEW MISSION: PROTECTING THE FUGITIVES

December 16, 2024

I've known for a while that this day would come, though I can't say I've ever felt truly ready for it. The crystal ball that I've kept so close, on my bookshelf, desk, dining room table, and wherever else I dared to put it, is finally going back into its box. I don't need it anyway. The Lost Souls can use the portal in my living room or the one in the upstairs guest bedroom. But it has shown me things I hadn't seen before. It also brought Candle Face and her Master Shadow deeper into my life, and the dread they've brought with them is something I can't live with anymore.

The Master Shadow already warned me that he'll return, and I know he doesn't need the crystal ball to do it. Still, the crystal ball has always felt like a beacon, or at least a focal point. If I take it out of my home, maybe I can dull his reach, even if only a little. Maybe I can slow him down, buy myself a little peace, or at least the illusion of it. Out of sight, out of mind.

I decided this afternoon to put it away. As I sat at my desk, the ball resting on its wooden stool, the silence in my home felt deafening. I lifted the ball and turned it slowly between my hands. A faint warmth radiated from it, unusual for a piece of glass that should have been at room temperature. My heart fluttered. Maybe this was a final parting shot, some remaining energy from the Master Shadow who had passed through it.

I took the crystal ball and lowered it toward its original box. That's when I noticed something strange. The ball reflected more than my anxious face. Inside, I saw shadowy figures. At first, they were just silhouettes. Human-shaped but featureless, perched on wooden beams and surrounded by what looked like pink insulation. My mind instantly went to the attic. Pink insulation, wooden beams. That's the space above my ceiling, right above my head.

I paused, holding the ball inches above the box. I tilted it slightly, and the angle changed the perspective of the shadows inside. More silhouettes came into view. There had to be around thirty of them, scattered along attic beams, huddled close, as if hiding from something. My pulse raced. I'd seen these shadow figures before and thought I recognized the area.

Yet I had no idea who they were or what they wanted. I knew only that my attic had become a refuge for something. Before I lowered the ball into the box, I took a deep breath and lifted it close to my face, studying these silhouettes, hoping to make out a clue. They moved slowly, shifting their weight on the beams, leaning into the insulation.

They seemed nervous and afraid. But afraid of what? Candle Face? The Master Shadow? Me?

I finally closed the box and set it aside. I couldn't just shove the crystal ball in the garage now, not after this. I had to confirm what I'd seen. My curiosity, dread, and sense of responsibility drove me upstairs. I climbed into the attic and turned on the overhead light. I looked around: dusty boxes and a huge HVAC system. Everything looked normal. No silhouettes. No movement. I waited at least ten minutes, listening to the hum of the HVAC system and the faint creaks of settling wood. If anyone or anything was up there, they stayed out of sight.

Eventually, I turned off the light and made my way back toward the crawl hole that leads into the guest room. The glow from the room guided my path, pale in the cramped attic. As I reached the opening and prepared to leave, I caught a glimpse. Two dark shapes darted behind the HVAC system. My heart slammed in my chest. So they were real.

Against my better judgment, I stayed in the attic and closed the doors behind me, blocking the guest room's light. After a minute, my eyes adjusted. I saw them again: one silhouette peeking around the HVAC unit, curious and cautious. I spoke quietly, telling it I wouldn't harm it. My voice sounded strange in the dark, and I hoped my wife wouldn't hear me. The silhouette vanished, then reappeared, as if weighing my intentions. I repeated my offer of peace.

Then more silhouettes rose into view. Heads popped up behind corners and beams. Shoulders emerged from shadows. I counted thirty of them, arranged in a loose circle around me. They seemed less frightened of me now. In the near-total darkness, they communicated through impressions and something close to telepathy. It felt as if their leader stepped forward, a shadow taller than the others, and projected its thoughts, its story, into my mind.

That's when I understood what had been happening. I didn't figure out their identity through intuition or guesswork. The leader told me directly. The apparitions were Lost Souls who had escaped Candle Face's Lair. That phrase, "Candle Face's Lair," filtered into my mind like a half-remembered thought. After all, I've seen that Lair with my own eyes twice. The leader filled my mind with images and emotions: the scorching horrors of that place and endless torment. My stomach churned with shock and empathy. They hadn't just wandered into my attic. They came here to hide.

The leader told me how they had used the portal in my guest room while other Lost Souls, the ones who appeared through my living room portal, risked themselves to distract Candle Face and her shadows. Those testimonies I've listened to, those flickering kitchen lights I've documented, were all part of a coordinated effort. The souls who visited me openly had bought time for these refugees to escape into my attic through the guest room portal.

So that's what all the flickering kitchen lights had been about. Each arrival of a lost soul, each strange surge of energy, matched the testimonies in my living room and the escapes through the guest room. The leader impressed on me that their combined energy was growing too strong to stay hidden for long. The Master Shadow would sense it, and he did, but he didn't look in the attic. He would return, just as he promised. And if he found them here, the punishment would be worse than anything they had already endured.

The leader's message was clear: they needed my help. They revealed themselves because they were desperate. They believed I could somehow protect them, shield them from detection, or help them stay hidden until they found a safer place. I wanted to protest that I was just an ordinary person and knew nothing about protecting spirits or Lost Souls. But how could I turn them away after learning their story?

Surrounded by their silhouettes, I felt terrified and responsible. I told them quietly, my voice steady despite what I was feeling, that I would do my best. I didn't know how, but I would try. The leader bowed its head slightly, a gesture of gratitude. The others looked on in silence. I could feel their fear, and I could feel the little bit of hope they had placed in me.

I understood their situation more deeply now. They had fled a place of unspeakable torment ruled by Candle Face. The Lost Souls who gave their testimonies in my living room had sacrificed their safety to buy these refugees time. Now all of that rested on my shoulders. If I fail to conceal or protect them, the whole operation collapses and these souls will be dragged back to endless suffering.

I started thinking through what I could do. Wards. Protective symbols. Maybe something to mask their combined energy. The crystal ball had perhaps made it easier for Candle Face's shadows to track my movements here, so putting it away might help. Even though the Master Shadow or Candle Face doesn't need the crystal ball to return, any step that weakens their foothold could help. I thought about folklore and old stories. Salt lines. Protective charms. Incantations. A friend of mine, Aaron, from Gen X Paranormal Investigations in Deer Park, Texas, conducts harvesting, which involves capturing and trapping spirits in boxes. He says he has many in his garage. I need to ask for his guidance. I need to try something.

Before I left the attic, I asked the leader silently if there were any instructions they could give me. The response came as a rush of impressions. "Hurry. Be discreet. Don't call unnecessary attention. The Master Shadow thrives on fear and detection." If I can keep these souls calm and their energy low, maybe he won't pinpoint their location. I wondered whether I should encourage them to spread through the attic, which is very large, or at least remain very still. But movement might stir up even more energy. They seemed to sense my struggle to form a plan and gave me one last plea. "Whatever you do, do it quickly."

I nodded and said I would return soon. Carefully, I edged backward, making my way to the attic doors. I opened them and climbed out into the guest bedroom. I retrieved the crystal ball box from my desk and carried it to the garage. I placed it high on a shelf. If the crystal ball served as a beacon, maybe this would stop it. Out of sight. Out of mind.

With that done, I went to my computer room to write this journal entry. I need to record these events and keep my thoughts organized. If I don't write it down now, I might convince myself it was some feverish dream. But no, it happened. I saw them, and they communicated with me. They trust me now. They depend on me.

It's strange how everything lines up. The flickering lights in my kitchen that used to puzzle me now make perfect sense. Every surge of energy, every trembling bulb, has matched new arrivals fleeing Candle Face's Lair. The Lost Souls using the living room portal had become allies of these attic refugees, knowingly putting themselves at risk to keep the Master Shadow occupied.

I just thought of something. Two Lost Souls yelled out, "Hide." They weren't warning me. They were shouting at the refugees. My chest tightened as the pieces clicked into place. "Hide" wasn't meant for me at all. It was for them. Of course.

Now it falls to me to repay their trust. I have to find a way. I've been around the paranormal long enough to know ignorance won't save me, the Lost Souls, or these refugees. I've read about protective herbs, about sigils drawn in chalk or etched into wood. I might try burning sage or placing salt lines along the attic's perimeter. Maybe I can arrange crystals, ordinary quartz or obsidian, to absorb or deflect their spiritual signatures. I'm grasping at straws without proper training, but I have to do something.

I can't stop thinking about the leader's fear. The Master Shadow can sense their combined presence. Time is short. He'll return, and when he does, he'll bring their doom unless I can hide them. I thought about reaching out to the souls who've given me testimonies in the living room. If I can summon one or two of them, I might learn more tricks of the trade. But summoning them risks more energy and more flickering lights, which might attract attention. It's a tightrope act with no net. Actually, I can't mention the refugees to the Lost Souls at all, because I know the shadows are listening when the Lost Souls are here. More than once, a lost soul has said something to me, and long arms came out of the portal and pulled the lost soul back in. So I mustn't mention the refugees to them.

I realize how serious my promise was. I told them I'd do my best. That means I can't sit idle. After finishing this journal entry, I'll try something simple. Maybe I'll place a ring of salt around the attic entrance. If folklore holds any truth, salt can create barriers or purify spaces. Even if it only calms my nerves while I think of a better plan, it may help. The key is to act fast and stay discreet. I mustn't let fear freeze me. Then again, if the Master Shadow comes back and sees the salt, that would be a dead giveaway. Maybe I don't leave any clues at all. Maybe I just need to figure out how to hide them. I don't have time for half-measures. They need me to act. Now.

Personal Note to My Readers

Please understand that the events leading up to tonight weren't random. The 14 months of Lost Souls' visits, the cryptic testimonies, the flickering lights, Candle Face's appearance, and the Master Shadow's threat were all building to this. I have around thirty escaped souls huddled in my attic, counting on me for their very existence. Failure means unimaginable torment for them, and likely for me too. The knowledge that I stood by and let it happen would stay with me forever.

At first, I called them escapees. That seemed to fit for a moment. Then I thought about calling them refugees. That didn't feel right either. These souls are being hunted. They're hiding. They're evading something that wants them back. The fear they carried moved through them as if the danger had followed them into the room. They ran as if what passed for their lives still depended on it. That's when it hit me: they were Fugitives.

The word fits because they're being pursued. They're hiding, surviving, trying not to be found. The danger is immediate. And now, by asking for my help, they've tied their fate to mine.

I hope I find a solution in time. Maybe this journal, this act of writing, will bring some clarity. Or maybe by the time I look back on these words, all will be lost. I can't let that happen. I have to be clever, resourceful, and compassionate. The Fugitives trusted me enough to tell me who they are and why they came. That trust is a gift and a burden. I have to honor it.

I'll start tonight. I'll contact my friend Aaron, and I'll dig deeper, maybe even find some obscure rituals online. I have to move quickly and quietly, just as they asked.

The Master Shadow will come. He said he would. When he does, I want him to find nothing out of place, no obvious beacon of escaped souls. I want him to pass us by, baffled and frustrated. If I can do that, I might buy these souls the time they need to stay free. And maybe I'll sleep a little easier, knowing I did my part.

CANDLE FACE CHRONICLES: THE MASTER SHADOW'S INSPECTION

December 22, 2024

The attic is quiet now. Too quiet. The Fugitives, thirty-one fragile souls who risked everything to escape Candle Face's Lair, are no longer scattered across the beams, hiding in the insulation. They are sealed now, each one contained in one of the small glass bottles I received from Amazon yesterday.

It wasn't a decision I made lightly. Aaron, from Gen X Paranormal Investigations, who specializes in spirit harvesting, suggested using specialized boxes to trap their energy safely. The boxes his team makes take time, sometimes weeks, sometimes months, but they're the best way to ensure spirits remain secure and undetectable. Unfortunately, time wasn't on my side. I needed something fast.

That's when I settled on glass bottles. They don't amplify energy like other materials, and they're easy to seal. I added glitter to the bottles as another layer of cover. It helped obscure the spirits' energy and made the bottles look like decorative trinkets, harmless and unassuming. It wasn't ideal, but it was the best solution I had with the time and resources available.

Getting the Fugitives into the bottles was easier than I expected, but emotionally grueling. I returned to the attic last evening, carrying the bottles in a padded case. Each one gleamed in the dim light, the curved surfaces reflecting faint rainbows. I placed the case on the attic floor and turned to face the leader of the Fugitives.

"You need to enter these," I said quietly, holding up a bottle. The leader studied it, the shadows of its form shifting uneasily. I could sense the doubt, the fear.

"They're safe," I added. "Glass will shield your energy. It's the only way to hide you from Candle Face and her Master Shadow. Once sealed, your energy won't combine with the others, which means it won't grow strong enough for them to sense. This is only a temporary solution, though," I continued, my voice soft but firm. "Once you're hidden, I'll distribute the bottles across the country. That way, your energy will stay scattered, far enough apart to keep you safe for now. Eventually, I'll figure out how to free you permanently."

One by one, the Fugitives moved toward the bottles. As each entered, their ghostly forms condensed into faint, swirling lights hidden among the glitter. I sealed the bottles tightly with a cork. Each seal shimmered faintly, a sign that the energy inside was stable.

When the final Fugitive entered a bottle, I stood there silently, staring at the row of containers. They looked so fragile, so small, yet they held the weight of thirty-one spirits who once lived among us.

I carried the bottles down to the garage and placed them carefully in the back of my car. For now, it seemed like the safest place. The Fugitives were hidden in plain sight. Now, I need to contact trusted friends and serious members of the paranormal community to see if they'd be willing to serve as guardians for these Fugitives until I determine how to free them permanently.

Just as I closed the trunk, the air in the garage grew hot. My breath caught in my throat. I knew what that meant. The Master Shadow was here.

He appeared in the doorway between the house and the garage, his form towering, dark, and shifting as though it were made of living smoke. The garage lights dimmed around him, as if his presence consumed the light itself. He stepped forward, his shadowy figure growing more solid with each movement.

I stepped away from the car and stood tall, hoping I looked brave in front of the Master Shadow, who could tear me to shreds.

"You think you've outsmarted me?" His voice was a low growl, vibrating through the air.

I froze, every instinct screaming at me to jump into the car, throw it in reverse, and smash through the garage door, but I forced myself to stand my ground. "There's nothing here for you," I said, my voice steadier than I felt.

His shadowed face tilted as if studying me, trying to see through me. Slowly, he moved deeper into the garage, his presence radiating unbearable heat. He brushed past the shelves, his smoky hands grazing random objects, but he didn't stop. My heart pounded as he neared the back of my car while I kept my mind clear just in case he could enter it.

He circled the vehicle, his form rippling like heat waves. He paused by the trunk, his hand hovering over the button to open it. I held my breath, every muscle tense, but he didn't open it. Instead, he turned back toward me, his shadowy face unreadable. Apparently, so was mine.

"There's nothing here," the Master Shadow said, though his tone carried a hint of doubt. "At least, not yet."

He stepped closer, his voice dropping to a hiss. "But you won't win this game. You can't save them all. And when I find them..." He leaned in, his face inches from mine. "...You think you're clever, but you've only delayed the inevitable. You can't protect them forever."

Forcing myself to meet his gaze, I said, "I'm not afraid of you, Kenneth McDuff."

The name hit him like a slap. His form wavered, the shadows rippling violently as though fighting to hold their shape. For a moment, I thought he might lash out, but instead, he let out a low, menacing laugh.

"So, you've solved the riddle," he said, his voice almost amused. "A name is a weapon, but it cuts both ways." He leaned in closer, his voice a deep growl. "But don't forget, every weapon can misfire."

"You should take your own advice," I shot back.

The Master Shadow laughed one final time. With that, he vanished, leaving the garage still. I leaned against the car, my legs trembling. Somehow, he knew I had the Fugitives nearby, but he couldn't find them.

His words shot back into my mind: "You can't save them all. And when I find them..." Did he know they had escaped Candle Face's Lair? Or was he guessing? His doubt gave me a slim advantage, but his confidence was unmistakable. The way he said "when I find them" instead of "if I find them" was a warning. He was certain the Fugitives couldn't stay hidden forever.

Personal Note to My Readers

I wondered briefly if this mistake could cost him something. The Master Shadow was responsible for overseeing the Lost Souls, wasn't he? Does Candle Face know she's missing some of them, or is he searching on his own without her knowing? If she doesn't know, maybe I could inform her, after I distribute the bottles, of course.

If I could exploit the division between Candle Face and the Master Shadow, pitting them against each other, it might buy me the time I need. This divide-and-conquer approach, what intelligence circles call 'exploiting internal divisions,' would be a dangerous gamble. But the stakes here were higher than any battlefield.

The thought of creating a wedge between them was tempting. If they turned against each other, maybe I'd have an advantage. But the risk was enormous. If she saw me as a threat, I'd be next in line for her wrath. But if I could make the Master Shadow her next target, it might be worth it.

Aaron mentioned that McDuff is buried in Huntsville, Texas, where he was executed in 1998. Dirt from his grave might hold some kind of connection to his spirit, a remnant of who he was in life. If I could use that, perhaps I could weaken him, or even bind him. The idea was tempting, but it would require careful planning and precision.

I was still thinking about it as I locked the house for the night. As I passed the hallway mirror, I caught a glimpse of my reflection. My face was pale, my eyes heavy with exhaustion, but my jaw was set. I looked drained and haunted, but I wasn't defeated. Not yet.

McDuff was tied to Candle Face's Lair, and he wasn't going to stop. The Fugitives had escaped, but he wouldn't rest until they were back. Everything had changed, and I knew I was in deeper than before.

TO BE CONTINUED...

The past 14 months have been filled with testimonies, hidden messages, and brief moments of understanding that often lead to more questions. Each spirit that has come to me has shared more than an isolated story. Each one has brought part of something larger, and it has grown more complex with every encounter. The Lost Souls have guided me this far, revealing their fears, their pain, and their need for justice. But now, as the Master Shadow's presence makes things ten times worse, I have to wonder: will more Lost Souls still seek my help, knowing the risk they face if discovered? Will their voices go silent, leaving their stories unfinished? Or will my work shift toward the fugitives, those fragile spirits who have managed to slip away from Candle Face's Lair? And if no new Lost Souls come, will the fugitives find me on their own?

The strain of this mission has never been greater, but abandoning it isn't an option. I've made a promise to help those who trust me with their stories. Still, I can't ignore the thought that it may be time to take a different approach. If no new spirits come forward, perhaps my focus must turn to Candle Face herself. Who was she before she became what she is now? What from her past might explain her power and offer a way to destroy her?

Aaron, the paranormal investigator from Gen X Paranormal Investigations, has supported me throughout this process. He believes that confronting Candle Face directly may be the way forward. He could be right, but I don't know yet. If we were to contain or destroy her, what would happen to those still trapped in her Lair? Would they remain there, lost forever? I can't risk taking that step without first helping them find freedom. It feels like the next chapter must begin with freeing her victims, even as I prepare to face her.

The future is unclear, and this story isn't finished. Whether it means finding peace for the fugitives, tracing the origins of Candle Face's power, or confronting her shadows, the investigation continues. Time will show what comes next.

To be continued…

THANK YOU!

Thank you for reading *Candle Face Chronicles: The Lost Souls [Book Two]*. I appreciate the time you spent reading this book. If you found it worthwhile, I'd be grateful if you took a few minutes to leave a review on Amazon (https://amzn.to/4bsM6ib). Even a short review helps. Reviews help a book find new readers, and I always appreciate hearing from readers. More readers mean a better chance of helping the Lost Souls.

Arthur M. Mills, Jr.

FOLLOW CANDLE FACE CHRONICLES ONLINE

- **Website: https://www.candleface.com**
  The central archive for the *Candle Face Chronicles* investigation.

- **Facebook: https://www.facebook.com/candlefacechronicles**
  Updates, findings, reader responses, and broader paranormal content beyond the core investigation.

- **YouTube: https://www.youtube.com/@CandleFace666**
  Video entries, readings, and case analysis.

- **Reddit: https://www.reddit.com/user/CandleFaceChronicles**
  A place for readers to help identify the Lost Souls, protect the Fugitives, and study Candle Face.

- **Medium: https://candlefacechronicles.medium.com**
  Longer journal entries and written case notes, often layered with clues.

www.ingramcontent.com/pod-product-compliance
Lightning Source LLC
Chambersburg PA
CBHW070916180626
46817CB00003B/1078